PUFFIN BOOKS

Published by the Penguin Group
Penguin Books Ltd, 80 Strand, London WC2R 0RL, England
Penguin Group (USA) Inc., 375 Hudson Street, New York, New York 10014, USA
Penguin Group (Canada), 90 Eglinton Avenue East, Suite 700, Toronto, Ontario, Canada M4P 2Y3
(a division of Pearson Penguin Canada Inc.)
Penguin Ireland, 25 St Stephen's Green, Dublin 2, Ireland (a division of Penguin Books Ltd)
Penguin Group (Australia), 250 Camberwell Road, Camberwell, Victoria 3124, Australia
(a division of Pearson Australia Group Pty Ltd)
Penguin Books India Pvt Ltd, 11 Community Centre, Panchsheel Park, New Delhi – 110 017, India
Penguin Group (NZ), 67 Apollo Drive, Mairangi Bay, Auckland 1310, New Zealand
(a division of Pearson New Zealand Ltd)
Penguin Books (South Africa) (Pty) Ltd, 24 Sturdee Avenue, Rosebank, Johannesburg 2196, South Africa

Penguin Books Ltd, Registered Offices: 80 Strand, London WC2R 0RL, England

penguin.com

Published 2006
1

Set in Times Ten by Palimpsest Book Production Limited, Stirlingshire

Made and printed in England by Clays Ltd, St Ives plc

British Library Cataloguing in Publication Data
A CIP catalogue record for this book is available from the British Library

ISBN-13: 978-0-141-32143-1
ISBN-10: 0-141-32143-1

HAPPY FEET

™

Novelization

Adapted by KAY WOODWARD

PUFFIN

In the velvety darkness of space, studded with sparkling stars, spins a blue and green planet covered in swirling clouds. If you travel through space towards the southernmost region of the planet, you will be surprised to find this place to be a freezing wasteland, completely blanketed in ice and snow. But here in the coldest, most dire conditions imaginable, you will discover the most remarkable and courageous nation of beings, who every year find renewed strength to hope, love and sing from their hearts. These are the Emperor penguins and the singing is their Heartsongs.

Chapter 1

Sometimes great things happen in the most ordinary of ways. It is said it all started one day during the season of love when the most sought-after penguin in Emperor Land, Norma Jean, sashayed across the smooth ice. She was singing her Heartsong in the hope of finding a mate, as is the way of the Emperor penguins. The problem was, now every male penguin was crooning his own tune back to her, which made things pretty noisy. How was she supposed to find her soulmate when she couldn't even *hear* above the hullabaloo?

'Boys, boys, *boys*!' she cried. 'Give a chick a chance!'

For a moment, all the males clustered

around her fell silent, gazing love-struck at the beautiful Norma Jean . . .

Then suddenly, a mesmerizing voice rang out across the ice shelf.

Slowly, she turned around.

And there he was. Tall and strong, with feathers as black as night and as white as snow, he came towards her, serenading her . . . melting her heart. He was handsome, regal and he knew how to wiggle his hips, which was definitely different! Norma Jean was smitten. She'd found him at last. And he'd found his soulmate.

As their two solo voices became a duet, their songs became love, and soon their love became the egg.

But all too soon it was fishing season, and the ice shelf was packed with penguins saying their tearful goodbyes. Memphis and Norma Jean lingered among them, reluctant to separate, but knowing that they must. Once their egg hatched, they knew their baby would be hungry.

So in the tradition of Emperor penguins, the mother left to hunt for fish in the deep waters far away, while the father stayed to do a most important job: to care for their one and only precious egg.

'If only you could stay a little, darling,' Memphis said wistfully.

'There are no fish on the ice,' replied Norma Jean softly. 'And you've got to stay here to do egg-time.'

Memphis sighed, but knew she was right. 'Give it to me, baby,' he said.

Slowly, but surely, Norma Jean passed over the egg. Memphis carefully tucked it on top of his feet and under his snuggly belly.

'Hold it tight, now,' said Norma Jean. 'Are you going to be OK . . . Daddy?'

'Sure, honey,' said Memphis bravely. He watched as she disappeared into the crowd of departing mother penguins. 'Goodbye, Norma Jean,' he called after her. 'Don't you worry about a thing. I'll keep him safe and warm till you get back!'

As the last rays of sun dipped below the horizon an inky blackness spilled across the sky.

It grew dark and bitterly cold. The icy winds whooshed and swirled, whipping snowflakes round the group of forlorn fathers. The long night of winter had begun.

Noah the Elder, the oldest and most respected penguin of them all, drew himself up to his full height. The Emperor penguins depended on him to bring focus to the community during these trialsome times. And Noah took on this responsibility with utter seriousness. 'When all the others leave . . .' he intoned.

'We remain,' Memphis and the other fathers chanted in reply, shivering as the wind grew stronger.

'When the sun vanishes . . .' Noah continued.

'We remain,' the fathers replied dutifully.

'Heed the wisdom, brothers!' boomed Noah above the sound of the howling gale. 'Make a huddle . . . warm thy egg.' The father penguins drew closer together, their eggs balanced on their feet.

'Share the cold!' Noah commanded. 'Each must take his turn against the icy blast if we are to survive the endless night!' Obediently, the penguins at the warm centre of the huddle peeled away to take the brunt of the wind, among them Memphis.

'Raise your voices, brothers!' roared Noah the Elder, his voice rising to an ear-splitting crescendo. 'Give praise to the Great Guin, who puts songs in our hearts and fish in our bellies!'

A towering swirl of snow formed above the huddle, creating a vision of the Great Guin giving forth a fountain of fish.

But Memphis wasn't thinking of the almighty Great Guin who took care of them all. He only had thoughts for Norma Jean. There she was, in his mind's eye, singing her own song in her irresistible voice. Absent-mindedly, he began to dance along to the song in his head with a shuffle here, a hip-wiggle there, until – *pop!* The egg shot out of its snug, safe place and rolled away into the blizzard!

'Whoa! NO! Oh nooo! No!' cried Memphis.

Desperately, Memphis rushed after the egg, slipping and sliding in his haste. Precious seconds passed – in another minute the egg would freeze. 'Arggghh,' he groaned, frantically scrambling about in the fresh snow. 'Is it here?

It could be here . . .' He found it half-buried in the swirling snow. With a sigh of relief, he grabbed the dear, darling egg and tucked it back into the warmth of his feathers.

'Shhhh . . . It's OK,' Memphis whispered, half to the egg, half to himself. 'There's no harm done, see?' He looked up nervously to see if anyone was watching as he quickly took his place back in the huddle. They weren't. 'We're . . . we're cool. Everything's gonna be just fine,' he muttered, knowing deep in his heart that there is no greater mistake than for an Emperor penguin to drop his egg.

Chapter 2

Of the thousands of voices chanting through the everlasting winter, Memphis sang the most fervently to the Great Guin to bring back the sun. At long last, the curtain of darkness lifted to reveal a vast, white, glittering world and Memphis's wait through the terrible winter was finally over. As the sun rose, the shadows shrank and the icicles melted in the spring sunshine. The ice shelf itself began to groan and moan and a great crack appeared. Soon, the whole expanse of winter ice had melted away.

Then . . . an egg cracked open. *CRAACKK!* And another egg! And another! Soon, all of Emperor Land was alive with hatching eggs. Sounds of rejoicing filled the air. The father penguins grinned with delight as fluffy chick after fluffy chick emerged, blinking, into the dazzling daylight.

'Hey, it's a girl!' cried one proud dad.

'It's a boy!' shouted another.

'What a peach!'

'What a bruiser!'

But Memphis stood apart, staring at his egg, lying grey and lifeless on the ice, waiting for a sign. Nothing.

Memphis's best friend, Maurice, came over with his hatchling, Gloria. 'Memphis?' he asked, concerned. 'Is . . . everything OK?'

Memphis could hardly speak. Was this because he dropped the egg? Was it *his* fault? 'Uh . . . I don't know,' he mumbled. 'I can't hear anything.'

'Sometimes the eggs don't make it,' said his friend kindly.

'I know,' Memphis said heavily.

They both stared at the egg, watching as Gloria tapped it with her beak. 'Is it empty?' she asked. 'Can I have it?'

'Gloria!' scolded Maurice.

But the little chick carried on with her

rhythmic tapping on the shell. *Tap-tap-tappity-tap-tap.*

'It's OK,' said Memphis miserably, his heart sinking.

'It happens sometimes,' said Maurice gently.

Gloria tap-tap-tappity-tapped again.

Then suddenly – the egg tapped back!

Memphis froze. 'Wait!' he said. 'Did you hear that?'

Gloria laughed gaily and tapped the egg again.

The egg replied. *Tap-tap-tappity-tap.*

'Hey, I can hear you!' Memphis shouted to the egg, hardly able to believe his ears. 'Your pappy's here!' He turned to Maurice, grinning broadly. 'He's OK!'

Crack. A tiny foot popped out of the egg. *Crack.* Then another. The egg performed a neat backflip, before landing on its feet and lurching off across the ice in a giddy, stumbling hippity-hop.

'Whoa, little buddy!' said Memphis. 'Slow down!'

At the sound of the muffled squawking coming from inside the egg, Gloria giggled.

'Come back here, Mr Mumble!' she said.

'Gloria . . .' began Maurice.

But Memphis didn't mind – he was just so relieved! His little egg was alive! 'She can call him whatever the heck she likes!' he said, rushing forward as the two-legged egg wobbled and almost tripped. 'Whoa, little Mumble!' he called. Yep, it was a catchy name, all right.

But the running egg was totally out of control by now, careering madly into a slippery dip and hitting a bump before – *wheeeee!* – briefly becoming airborne and then landing hard. At once, the egg split open with a loud *CRAAAACK*, neatly depositing the fluffy chick on the ice.

'Are you OK, son?' asked Memphis, as the baby penguin hopped from one foot to another.

'Freezy, f-f-freezy!' Mumble gasped as his feet touched the cold ice.

Memphis chuckled. 'Oh, you'll get used to it,' he said. 'Come on, son. Come to your daddy!'

The other Emperor penguins watched curiously as Mumble hippity-hopped over to Memphis.

'Hey, what do you make of that?' said one penguin.

'A little wobbly in the knees, huh?' said another.

'What are you doing there, boy?' asked Memphis nervously.

'I'm happy, Pa,' Mumble said, hippity-hopping all over the ice.

By now, even more penguins were staring and Memphis was becoming concerned. What would they say if they thought Mumble was different? 'I wouldn't do that around here, son,' he said quietly.

'Why not?' asked Mumble, who was so happy that his feet just wouldn't keep still.

'Well, it just ain't penguin, OK?' said Memphis.

'OK, Pa,' said Mumble. With difficulty, he stopped dancing.

'Now, come on over here and get warm,' Memphis said.

Mumble didn't have to be asked twice, and he charged towards Memphis. 'Watch the beak!' cried Memphis as his son headed straight between his feet. 'Watch the beak . . . Owww!'

Memphis looked nervously around.

The other penguins had stopped staring – at least for now.

Chapter 3

The days grew longer and the icy winds softened. All of Emperor Land eagerly awaited the mothers' long-anticipated return from fishing. Mumble perched on Memphis's feet, which were *much* warmer than the ice – as did thousands of other chicks with their dads. They all stared expectantly across the vast whiteness, waiting for the mothers' arrival. Days passed, but still no sign.

On an icy overhang far above, the Elders – the oldest, wisest penguins of them all – scanned the horizon.

'So late?' asked one of the Elders, Eggbert. 'What's keeping them?'

Noah puffed out his chest and looked solemn. 'Pray, brothers, that the Great Guin does not test us with a lean season. Are there any among us that have not been dutiful?'

Meanwhile, down below in the crowd of waiting fathers, Memphis had his own concerns. What would Norma Jean think when she saw Mumble's strange hippity-hop? He needed to make sure his son knew exactly what to do when Norma Jean arrived. 'So when you see your mama . . . ?' he prompted.

'I stand perfectly still,' Mumble replied.

'You got it.'

'But how will I know which one's my mama?' asked Mumble.

'Well . . .' For a moment, Memphis was lost for words. How could he describe the most wonderful penguin he'd ever met? 'She's got a wiggle in her walk,' he said at last, 'and a giggle in her talk. And when she sings, it darn near breaks your heart.'

Suddenly, a voice boomed across Emperor Land.

'Wives hooooooo! Wives hooooooo!'

Across the distant horizon, the familiar figures emerged. The mothers had returned!

In his excitement, Mumble instantly forgot

everything he'd been told and bolted towards the crowd of returning penguins.

'Wait, no . . . wait, Mumble!' Memphis shouted. 'Get back here, boy! Mumble! *Mumble!*' But he was nowhere near fast enough. Mumble was already lost in the crush of happy reunions.

'Roxanne!'

'Barbara Ann!'

'Alfie?'

'Delilah!'

'Mama!' Mumble cried, hoppity-skipping through the crowd.

Memphis careered after his eager son. 'Excuse me. Pardon me,' he apologized to Maurice, Michelle and Gloria on the way. 'Mumble! Where are you?'

Everywhere, families were being reunited. But Memphis was scurrying about, frantically searching for his son. Then, a familiar voice, as sweet as honey and as smooth as silk, flowed through the crowd.

'Memphis . . . ?'

He turned. There she was – his Norma Jean. One of the very last to arrive. 'Oh, Mama,' he sighed. She looked even more beautiful than he remembered.

'Oh, Daddy!' she smiled, wearing an expectant expression. 'So ... where's the baby?'

Memphis looked shifty. 'Well, honey ...' he began. 'I'm, ah ... I'll find him!'

'You *lost* the baby!' Norma Jean cried in disbelief. 'Memphis!'

But in the next moment, Memphis was saved by the sound of a tiny, excited voice – 'Mama!' shouted Mumble happily as he hippity-hopped towards them.

'Come to Mummy!' called Norma Jean.

'We'll come to *you*!' insisted Memphis. First, he needed to explain to Norma Jean that their son was a little *different*. But it was too late. The pitter-pat-pat-pattering of tiny feet was heading their way.

'Wha-what's wrong with his feet?' Norma Jean exclaimed.

'Oh, uh, that's just a little thing he's got going,' stammered Memphis. 'He'll grow out of it.'

But Memphis needn't have worried. There

was no way that Norma Jean could resist her fluffy little ball of laughter. She and Mumble twirled around each other, the happy chick hugging her leg to stop himself from whirling away across the ice.

'Oh, Memphis,' she said adoringly. 'He's *gorgeous*!'

'Isn't he, though?' agreed Memphis, heaving a huge sigh of relief.

Norma Jean bent down towards her little chick. 'Look at you,' she crooned. 'Close your eyes . . . open up. Mama's got a little something for you . . .' And she opened her beak and sent a stream of tasty fish bits – which she'd digested earlier – into his waiting mouth.

I love the way she does that, thought Memphis adoringly.

She turned towards Memphis. 'It looks like we may be facing a lean season, Daddy. We had to travel far and wide to find the fish.'

'Don't you fret, Norma Jean,' said Memphis. 'As long as all three of us are together, everything's gonna be just fine.'

Chapter 4

Soon, it was the very first day of term, and Miss Viola looked around at her class of fluffy penguin chicks. 'Today, we begin with the most important lesson you will ever learn.' She paused dramatically. 'Does anyone know what that is?' She waited for a reply. 'Anyone . . . ? Someone . . . ?' She looked around for a victim, her eyes resting on the largest chick in the class. 'Seymour?'

'Fishing?' Seymour said.

Heads turned as the littlest penguin of all hippity-hopped into the class.

'No,' said Miss Viola. She pointed to the late arrival. 'Mumble?'

'Um . . .' Mumble tried quickly to think of an answer. 'Don't eat yellow snow?' he suggested hopefully.

'No, that's not it . . .' sighed Miss Viola.

Gloria waved her flipper in the air. 'It's our Heartsongs, Miss,' she said, proudly.

The teacher smiled broadly. 'Thank you, Gloria,' she said. 'Excellent. Yes, without our Heartsongs, we can't be truly *penguin*, can we?'

'Noooo,' everyone chanted in unison, shaking their heads.

'But, my dears,' said Miss Viola, 'your Heartsongs are not something that I can actually teach you. Does anybody know why?'

Gloria waved her flipper again. 'You can't teach them to us, ma'am, because we have to find our Heartsongs all by ourselves. It's the voice you hear inside. The voice of who you truly are.'

'Exactly,' concluded Miss Viola. 'Thank you. So . . .' She stopped for a moment and looked around the excited faces of her class. 'Let's all be very still now. Take a moment and let it come to you.'

The little penguins fell silent, concentrating on their inner songs. Then all at once, there was a clamour of eager voices.

'I've got one!'

'Me!'

'Pick me! Choose *me*!'

'One at a time,' said Miss Viola. 'Yes . . . Seymour?'

Mumble watched, awestruck, as Seymour strutted to the front of the group and performed an expert rap.

Miss Viola guffawed. 'Yes, I like that one,' she said, wiggling in time to the beat. 'I could really get jiggy with that. Lovely.'

'I'm ready!' called Gloria. 'I've got one.'

'Ah . . . I thought you might.' Miss Viola smiled, nodding for her to continue.

Gloria stepped to the front. She closed her eyes, took a deep breath and opened her little beak to sing the most enchanting and beautiful melody. Her pure, clear voice echoed far across the ice. All across Emperor Land, penguins stood still to listen, utterly entranced.

Abruptly, Gloria finished. 'That's as far as I've got,' she said shyly.

'Lovely,' smiled Miss Viola. 'Really lovely.'

'That's beau-ti-ful,' breathed Mumble. He had never heard anything so wonderful in all his life.

The teacher's eyes locked on to him. 'Well,

Mumble,' she said. 'Since you seem so keen to share . . .'

Mumble hoppity-skipped to the front of the class, exchanging glances with Gloria as they passed each other. He couldn't help noticing that she looked concerned. But he wasn't worried. Mumble knew that his voice was kind of different and he liked it that way. 'Um . . . mine's sort of a *boom*,' he squawked, 'and a . . .' Here, he blew a series of wet, noisy raspberries. 'And another *boom*!' he finished.

There were sniggers and titters.

Miss Viola looked nonplussed. 'You heard that in *there*?' she asked, placing her flipper over her heart.

'Do you like it?' asked Mumble eagerly. He knew it wasn't your everyday, run-of-the-mill Heartsong, but it was the best he could do, and he was proud of it.

'Dear,' said Miss Viola very slowly, as if she were speaking to someone who was a little hard of hearing, 'I'm afraid that's not even a tune.'

'It's not?' said Mumble, confused.

'No, dear,' Miss Viola continued. 'A tune is like, um . . . la-la-la-la-la-laaaah.' She trilled a range of notes that lifted high before tumbling down low again.

'Oh, OK!' said Mumble brightly. So *that* was a tune. It sounded *so* easy. '**La**laaaLAHHHla **laaahhh**laAlaaaa!' he caterwauled.

The class spluttered with laughter at the awful noise, which was so loud and grating that it reached the ears of Noah and the Elders.

'Now, who is *that*?' demanded Noah.

'That is the offspring of Memphis and Norma Jean,' Eggbert answered.

'Ahhh . . .' said Noah, as if this explained everything. 'The wee hippity-hopper.'

Across the ice, the squawking continued.

'La la **la** LaaaA **la** laa laAAAAAA-HHHH!' hollered Mumble, the sound of his voice dislodging icicles dangling above him. They clinked to the ground, one landing squarely on his head.

Everyone laughed hysterically – except Gloria. 'It's not funny!' she protested loudly.

'No,' Miss Viola said gravely, 'not in the least. A penguin without a Heartsong –' she looked soberly at Mumble – 'is hardly a penguin at all.'

Chapter 5

Miss Viola broke the bad news to Memphis and Norma Jean straight away. The teacher leaned forward confidentially. 'In all my years, I've never –' She broke off and tried again. 'I mean . . . and you having such fine voices. Well, it's bizarre.' She glanced across at Mumble, who was splashing happily in a meltwater pool a little distance away, then looked back at his parents. 'Did anything happen, you know, during early development?'

'No, all fine,' said Norma Jean. 'Normal incubation, wasn't it, honey?'

Memphis paused. The memory of the dropped egg came flooding to him. Could Mumble's weirdness with the feet be his fault? But how could he possibly admit this in front of everyone? Memphis gave a nervous nod. 'Yeah . . .' he lied. 'It was a tough winter, I guess. And he – he did hatch a little late . . .'

'Yes, I understand,' Miss Viola sympathized.

Norma Jean gazed at Mumble, at a complete loss. 'To think that he might spend his life alone . . . never to meet his one true love.' It was true. Without a Heartsong, how could anyone fall in love with Mumble?

By now, Memphis's expression was totally guilt-stricken. 'Oh, please, Miss Viola,' he implored. 'Isn't there *something* we can do?'

The teacher was thoughtful. 'Well, there is always . . . Mrs Astrakhan,' she encouraged. 'If anyone can, Mrs Astrakhan can,' she said, pointing towards a large ice cave in the distance.

'Can't sink?' roared a rather large Mrs Astrakhan. 'Can't *sink*? Rubbeesh, darlink! Every little pengvin has a sonk.' She smiled encouragingly. 'Ven I have feenished, your singink vill be givink everyone the goosepimpel.'

Memphis and Norma Jean watched anxiously

from a short distance away. If Mrs Astrakhan could work her magic, they would surely be the happiest penguins in the world.

'Now, to begin,' said Mrs Astrakhan. 'First, ve must find a feelink. Happy feelink, sad feelink . . . maybe *lonely* feelink. You feel it?' asked Mrs Astrakhan.

'I do!' said Mumble, excitement rising inside him.

'Good,' Mrs Astrakhan said delightedly. 'Now let it out. Be *spontaneous*!'

Mumble felt a momentary rush of happiness flood through him, warming him all the way to his feet – and he suddenly let go! *Tippity-tap-tap-tap. Tip-tappity-hop-hop.*

'Vat!' cried Mrs Astrakhan. 'Vat is *that*?'

Mumble looked from the teacher to his parents. They all wore concerned looks, and he didn't know why. What was the problem? 'I'm being spon-tan-uous,' he explained.

Mrs Astrakhan tried again. 'Darlink, you vant to meet beautiful girl?'

'Mmm-hmm,' replied Mumble.

'You vant to make the egg?'

'Oh, yes.'

'Vell sink!' she roared. 'And no jiggy-jog. Do not move muscle. *No movink!*'

So Mumble sang. 'Twi*ink*Le, **twi***i*inkle, *litt*le STaAR!'

'Enough!' said Mrs Astrakhan, her face horrified. 'Ve go back to the top. Forget body . . . look inside the *soul*. Feel the feelink. *Enormous* feelink. So enormous eet fills whole body. It must escape or you *explode*! Now, open your leetle beak and . . . *now*!'

Mumble opened his beak, took a deep breath – closed his eyes and listened deep within himself. Slowly, he felt his feet start to move, first one, then the other. Then they started to tap – faster and faster! Soon they were flying across the ice, tapping out exquisite rhythms that spread joy from the bottom of his heart to the very tip of his toes. Never in his life had Mumble felt so excited, so happy. The song in his heart was at last *free*.

I did it! he thought, proudly, gasping for breath. But what was this? Mrs Astrakhan had collapsed on the ice!

'Disaster!' the teacher sobbed. 'Catastroff! I never fail before – *never*!'

But Mumble didn't understand what all the fuss was about. He had done exactly what he was supposed to do. How could dancing bring him such sheer and utter happiness, but upset and frustrate everyone else?

It was all too much for Memphis. The lesson had been an utter failure. Could it be possible that Mumble's *thing* with the feet was somehow *his* fault? He shook his head. Even so, Mumble would have to learn to behave like everyone else. This strange hippity-hop must *stop*.

'Well I thought it was kinda cute,' ventured Norma Jean, interrupting his thoughts as they hurried away. 'So what if he's a little different? I always kind of liked *different*.'

'He's *not* different,' Memphis snapped. 'He's a regular Emperor penguin, do you hear me?'

'Hey,' Mumble butted in. He didn't know what the problem was – *he* didn't mind being different. 'I can leave school! I can go to work!'

Memphis stopped and faced his son. 'Whoa!' he said. 'You ain't going nowhere till you've got yourself an education. Get those singing muscles big and strong, you got that?'

'I'll try, Pa,' mumbled Mumble.

'You bet you will,' replied his father sternly. 'The word "triumph" starts with "try" and ends with – UMPH!' Memphis said, with a deft move of his hips.

'Umph,' said Mumble, copying his dad's cool hip move. Umph. Umph. Umph.

Chapter 6

Things weren't going well on the ice shelf. Fish were scarce, which meant that the adult penguins had to put in a whole lot of overtime trekking to the sea and back, searching for precious food. But it also meant that Mumble had time when he could escape the notice of the other penguins' tutting and sighing, and let his happy feet go *really* wild. High up on the ice shelf, far away from the disapproving eyes of the community, he was free to hippity-hop and tippity-tap his way to and fro across the ice. It was only when he was dancing that he felt truly alive, and, in his absolute bliss, he often didn't notice where he was or what was around him . . . or the dark, looming shadow that was flitting overhead.

Suddenly, in mid-spin, Mumble found himself face to face with a mean-looking skua.

'Hey, whatcha doin' there, flipper-bird?' the skua squawked, towering over the little penguin.

'Nothing,' Mumble replied automatically. 'What are *you* doing?'

'Nothin' . . . Just dropped in for a little lunch,' said the skua airily, as three more skuas landed with a rush of flapping wings.

'There's food?' asked Mumble. 'Here?' His empty tummy began to rumble loudly at the thought. The birds cackled, their dark, beady eyes fixed on Mumble. Feeling uneasy, he backed away.

'Hmmm . . .' said the chief skua. 'Leg or wing?'

'No!' shouted Mumble, suddenly realizing that *he* was the food. 'Not me. I'm a *penguin*.'

'Exackly,' said the skua greedily. 'De flipper-birds – dat's *you* – eat de fish. De flying birds – dat's *me* – eat de flipper-bird *and* de fish. And lately, there ain't a lotta fish, so . . .' He moved towards Mumble. His three hungry compatriots were close behind, arguing over who would get the juiciest bits.

'Wait!' cried Mumble, thinking on his feet. 'Watch this!' And he performed a speedy tap dance, hoping desperately this would distract the birds from their thoughts of penguin supper.

It didn't.

'Yeah, dat's weird awright,' the skua agreed as he pushed Mumble to the icy ground, putting a huge claw on his chest. He opened his beak to strike and –

'What's that?' Mumble asked, trying again to distract the skua. He pointed at the yellow band around the skua's leg. It was made of a strange material.

The skua chief stopped in his tracks. 'What? This li'l ting?' he said, lifting his foot. Mumble took the opportunity to scramble to his feet.

'No! No!' cried the other birds. 'Don't start 'im on that!'

'Shut up!' squawked the leader. 'The li'l flipper-bird asked me a perceptive question – a question that desoives an answer.'

One of the other birds rolled his eyes. 'Here we go . . .' he muttered.

The skua fixed Mumble with a crazy, bloodshot eye. 'I got two words for ya,' he said.

'*Alien Abduction*.' He ruffled his wings importantly. 'Now, li'l buddy. Dere's somethin' out dere. Creatures. Not like us. Bigger . . . fiercer . . . an' smarter too. Ask me 'ow I know.'

'How?' said Mumble obligingly.

'I'm sittin' on a rock, mindin' me own business,' said the skua, 'when suddenly, dere onta me! Dese bein's are like big, ugly penguins . . . fat, flabby faces with frontways eyes, no feathers, no beaks . . . an' dese . . . dese . . . appendages! Dey probe me, dey tie me up and strap me down . . . dey take dis pointy ting and stick it inta me! And den . . . blackout!'

'Gosh,' said Mumble, playing for time.

'I woke up with dis *ting* on me,' continued the skua, waving his bracelet, 'and every flyin' bird is dissin' me, calling me Yellaleg – it's *humiliatin*'!'

'And then what?' asked Mumble. He looked frantically for a way to escape.

The skua was indignant. 'What more d'ya want?'

'They could have eaten you,' Mumble suggested helpfully.

'Yeah . . .' agreed the skua. 'I guess my

pitiful cries for moicy appealed to their better nature.'

Mumble took his chance. 'Can I appeal to *your* better nature?' he asked hopefully.

'Nice try, kid,' said the skua, his eyes hard. 'But . . . no.'

The skuas headed menacingly towards Mumble, who stumbled backwards.

'No, nooo – whooaa!' he cried, falling into a narrow crevice between two ice ledges. He tumbled to the bottom and cowered just out of reach. The hungry skuas tried to jab at him with their beaks, desperate for food. Meals were few and far between and who knew when their next meal might come? After only getting beakfuls of Mumble's downy fluff, the birds knew they were beaten, and they flew away, disgruntled.

The little chick sobbed with relief, shaken and alone.

But still he had questions. Who were these Aliens? And what fabulous creatures and strange worlds lay out there, far beyond the ice? Could one small penguin ever hope to know?

Chapter 7

After the skua attack, Mumble never danced alone again. Instead, he spent the rest of his schooldays at the back of the class with his beak tightly shut, daydreaming of the world beyond the ice shelf.

Days turned into weeks and the penguin chicks grew. Soon, their downy feathers tumbled away to reveal the sleek, black and white Emperor penguins beneath. They were tall, elegant adults, ready to graduate. All except poor Mumble, who was the only one with grey baby fluff still clinging to his coat.

Noah the Elder addressed the eager penguins from his icy podium. 'A thousand generations ago, our forefathers forsook our wings for flippers. You graduates, going to sea for the first time, are to reap the benefits of their wise choice.' He paused and looked over the assembled crowd. 'These are lean and uncertain times, but by the power of the ancient Penguin Wisdoms, we will endure!'

A wave of applause rolled through the crowd.

'My fellow Emperors,' Noah droned on. 'No matter how far you stray from the security of our homeland, stay true to our ways . . .'

'Blah blah blah . . .' said Norma Jean.

'Shush!' Memphis scolded her in hushed tones.

'Who is he to say that my boy can't graduate?' said Norma Jean crossly. She smiled at Mumble, who stood apart from the others. 'He's not hurting anyone.'

'. . . and you will always be worthy of this,' said Noah, who still wasn't finished, 'our brave Penguin Nation. Excelsior!'

The graduates tossed the last of their baby fluff into the air and cheered noisily. 'Excelsi-yah-yah-yah!' Full of hopes and dreams, they headed for the sea.

Mumble watched them wistfully.

'You know what?' said his mother. 'We're going to have a little graduation ceremony of our own.' Ignoring Memphis's shocked expression, she picked up a handful of fluff from the ground and gave it to Mumble, who grinned delightedly.

Whoosh! Norma Jean and Mumble hurled fluff just like the real graduates. 'Excelsi-yah-yah-yah!' they cried.

'Shhh!' hushed Memphis, checking furtively to see if anyone was watching.

'Pa, come on,' said Mumble, his eyes imploring Memphis to join in. He so wanted his father to be proud of him.

'Er . . . Yah-yah-yah,' Memphis muttered.

'Yeah!' cheered Mumble. And he hippity-hopped after the departing penguins, his parents' cries ringing in his ears.

'Go get 'em, tiger!' called Norma Jean. 'Make every moment count!'

'Don't go out too far, little buddy,' warned Memphis. 'Watch out for those Leopard seals and killer whales!'

'I knew it from the start,' Eggbert the Elder muttered to Noah, as they watched Mumble skip-hop into the distance. 'That boy was always a bad egg. I'm telling you, no good will come of this!'

Meanwhile, Mumble's old classmates gathered nervously at the edge of a large glacier, gazing down at the dark blue water below.

'You first,' said one.

'Are you kidding?' said another.

No one was game to take the plunge.

Except Mumble! He was growing more and more excited. The sea was in sight! He threw himself on to his belly and careered towards the huddle of graduates. 'Watch your backs!' he cried. 'Coming through!' The crowd scattered and Mumble – going so fast by now that everything was a blur – launched off the edge of the cliff. He tumbled, he spun and finally – *kersplash!* – he hit the water.

There was a long silence, as the graduates craned over the edge, looking for a glimpse of the reckless penguin.

Suddenly, Mumble shot out of the water like a cannonball. 'What are you waiting for?' he cried. 'It's fantastic!' And he disappeared below the surface again. Now that they could see how easy it was, the rest of the penguins followed suit, whooping and hollering as they plunged towards the icy water.

Mumble ducked below the surface again. He couldn't believe how much fun it was being underwater – and when he heard a familiar voice, his heart fluttered.

'Mumble?' asked Gloria uncertainly.

'Gloria?' he replied.

She had grown into a sleek and beautiful penguin. Shyly, they swam around each other, and Mumble tried to summon the courage to say what he really felt. 'Gloria,' he began. This was it. He was going for it. 'All my life, I've wanted to say that y-you're so –'

'Fish?' Gloria butted in.

Mumble wasn't entirely sure that this was what he'd had in mind, but he nodded anyway. 'Y-yeah,' he said. 'You're so . . . fish.'

'No!' shouted Gloria. 'Fish!' She pointed excitedly to a small school of fish a little way off.

'FISH!' cried all the other penguins.

It was every penguin for himself. Hundreds

of penguins from everywhere zoomed eagerly after the little shoal, the water a whirl of frantic flippers, snatching and grabbing until every tasty morsel was gone.

Mumble swam up to Gloria, proudly displaying his catch. 'Did you get one?' he asked, which was not an easy thing to do with a mouthful of fish.

'Nope,' said Gloria sadly. 'Not this time.'

Mumble couldn't bear to see her so disappointed. '*You* have it,' he said.

'Thank you, but it's yours,' replied Gloria, with a kind smile. 'You caught it. You eat it.'

'I want *you* to have it,' said Mumble stubbornly. 'Take it!' *Whoosh!* In the blink of an eye, a sneaky skua swooped down and snatched the fish from Mumble's mouth. *Peeoww!* Mumble torpedoed out of the water after him, gripping the skua, his weight dragging the large bird downwards. Mumble struggled to grab the fish, but another skua clamped on – and still a third one joined in the battle! Flapping madly, the three birds gained height, taking the fluffy penguin with them.

'Mumble! Let go!' cried Gloria.

But, like a dog with a very juicy bone, Mumble held on to his fish. The skuas flew higher and higher, over the ice now, until . . . the fish tore in half! Mumble plummeted through the air with the other half of the fish still in his beak and hit the ice with a loud, hard *smack*!

Gloria jumped out of the water and rushed over. 'Are you OK?' she asked worriedly.

Mumble groaned and opened one eye. 'Take . . . the . . . fish,' he said wearily.

Gloria swallowed it in one dainty gulp. She looked at the exhausted Mumble with new eyes, and, for the very first time, thought, *Maybe . . . just maybe, Mumble might actually be the one*.

That night, the graduates celebrated atop a tall glacier, gathering together for the evening's extravaganza. The shining star of the night was Gloria. Against the glimmering Southern Lights, she sang one of the loveliest songs Emperor Land had ever heard. The penguins swayed back and forth, mesmerized by her tune. Mumble himself was so overcome by the beauty of her voice that he lifted his head to join in, barely aware that he had starting singing. 'AYEEEEahhhooooEEEeeeeaaah-HHHH!' The whole concert screeched to a halt. The mood was shattered. 'What's wrong with you?' shouted a penguin. 'Keep it down, weirdo!'

'You're spoiling it for everyone,' grumbled another.

Gloria's voice rose above the jeers and catcalls. 'Mumble,' she said kindly. 'Maybe you'd better just . . . you know . . . listen.'

'I know,' Mumble said heavily, feeling utterly alone. He trudged away into the darkness, discovered a floating ice pad and climbed on to it. As he floated away, he could still hear Gloria's beautiful voice, echoing across the endless night. *At least I can enjoy her song now without ruining it for everyone else*, he thought before drifting off into a fitful sleep.

Chapter 8

The next morning, Mumble's ice floe had drifted far away from Emperor Land. He was woken with a jolt. Mumble looked around sleepily. 'OK, fellers,' he said. 'Cut it out.' He peered over the side of his icy raft and saw nothing but slowly spreading ripples. Another violent nudge almost threw Mumble into the sea.

'Ha ha,' said Mumble unenthusiastically. 'I'm completely terrified.' Why couldn't they just leave him alone? He peered over the side, saw a dark shape hurtling his way and his stomach turned over. 'Gloria?' he said weakly. 'Guys?'

Gaping jaws lurched out of the water, missing Mumble by a whisker. 'Aaaarghhh!' he cried, frantically scrambling away from the murderous Leopard seal and tumbling into the water. Thrashing wildly in terror, Mumble made for a nearby ice shelf, clambering to safety just in time. But the deadly creature swam under the ice and blasted through it with brute force. Mumble was flung into the water once more.

There was only one place left for him to hide – the bottomless depths of the ocean. He swam for his life, darting and zigzagging through ever-narrowing corridors of ice, but wherever he went, his pursuer followed. *Chomp!* The Leopard seal clamped his razor-sharp teeth on to Mumble's tail, but the penguin pulled away, leaving a mouthful of feathers in his pursuer's mouth.

Mumble was beginning to lose all hope, when, out of the corner of his eye, he glimpsed a tiny shaft of light. The surface! He went for it, swimming at breakneck speed through a tunnel of ice, and zoomed towards the surface, jaws snapping just behind him until – *bam!* – he exploded into fresh air, closely followed by the Leopard seal.

Performing a neat flip, Mumble landed

elegantly on his feet and glided across the ice towards a bunch of Adelie penguins. They cheered noisily as the Leopard seal crashed through the ice hole and landed in a great, ungainly bellyflop.

'Yeah – safe!' one of them shouted to Mumble, who couldn't help noticing that the penguin had a strange accent. 'That's a nine point eight!'

'I give ju ten!' said another.

The Leopard seal lunged at the penguins, but fell well short. Mumble watched in amazement as the Adelies – who were about half his size, and wearing cool, tufty hairstyles – took turns taunting the huge Leopard seal, who might be slick and speedy underwater, but was a great, lumbering oaf on land. 'Over here!' they teased. 'Come on! Bring it on!'

The Leopard seal fixed on Mumble with a steely eye. 'Come here, sausage,' he threatened. 'I take you with ketchup!'

'But first ju've got to *catch up*!' said the smallest penguin of all, laughing uproariously at his own joke.

'Oh, here he comes,' one Adelie said,

watching the seething seal. 'We'd better move . . . *in half an hour*!'

They all roared with laughter.

'*Ay, caramba*. Let's . . . get . . . out . . . of . . . here,' added another, speaking and moving in exaggerated slow motion.

His recent terror quite forgotten, Mumble joined in the hilarity. Just out of reach of the Leopard seal's furious glare and enormous jaws, he tippity-tapped a defiant dance.

Immediately, the Adelies were entranced. 'Hey, *amigo*, do that again!' they cried.

'Do what?' asked Mumble.

'The clickety-clickety thing with the feet!'

'Oh, that,' said Mumble. 'Well, I just kind of go . . .' A little self-consciously now, he performed some extra steps.

'Oh, yeah! I like that! Nice,' said one of the Adelies appreciatively.

'And then this . . .' said Mumble, hardly able to believe that no one was laughing at him. Bolder now, he tippity-tappity-tip-tapped some more.

'Oooh, wow!' The little penguins applauded rapturously. 'Way to go, *el maestro*!'

With everyone engrossed in Mumble's tap-dancing, the Leopard seal made one last attempt at capturing lunch. He heaved his great body across the ice, aiming for the performing penguin, just falling short and landing – *splat!* – on his face.

The Adelies fell about laughing.

Enough was enough. The Leopard seal made its weary way back to the water, stopping only to mutter, 'Remember, dumplings, I know where you live.'

'Yeah, it's called "land", Lardface!' the Adelies guffawed. 'Flop back any time, Rubberbutt!' They turned to go, still chuckling.

Emboldened by his tap-dancing success, Mumble added a cautious retort to the seal as well: 'See you, Fatty.'

This stopped the Adelies in their tracks. 'All right!' said the smallest penguin, who seemed to be in charge. 'Way to go, Tall Guy!' Then they went on their way, trying out Mumble's moves.

Mumble watched as the Leopard seal slipped back into the water and realized that he was alone on the ice. He was suddenly nervous. What was he to do now? Was it safe to go back in the water?

'Oi!' shouted the bossy Adelie from the top of a snowy rise. 'Ain't ju coming, Tall Boy?'

'Um . . .' mumbled Mumble.

'What? You got something better to do?' asked the penguin.

Mumble thought for a moment. He looked out across the sea ice, floating endlessly to the horizon. In that direction was the world from which he'd come – a world where he didn't belong. He made up his mind. 'No,' he said. He didn't have anything better to do.

'Well then, come on with us to Adelie Land!' they cried.

Chapter 9

The Adelies – Nestor, Lombardo, Rinaldo, Raul and their leader, Ramon – took Mumble back to their colony. He couldn't believe his eyes. The valley was filled with thousands upon thousands of Adelies, stretching as far as the eye could see. All of them laughing and jumping, they whooped and danced to a cacophony of crazy rhythms and toe-tapping beats. Mumble was amazed. They were so different from the Emperor penguins, in both looks and attitude. And *he* was so different from the Adelies. But that didn't seem to matter to them! They liked him because he *was* different.

'Hey, Stretch,' cried Nestor. 'Ju like to party?'

'Party?' asked Mumble. Partying wasn't something that he did back home exactly, but . . . 'I guess so,' he ventured.

'Well, stick with us,' said Nestor.

'Everyone's so . . . spon-tan-uous,' said Mumble, totally overwhelmed by it all.

The Adelies shook with laughter. '*Si*,' Rinaldo agreed. 'And these are bad times! Our food chain's gone loco, but it ain't gonna stop no party!'

'Gosh,' said Mumble, as a penguin sauntered past with a pebble in his beak. Things certainly were different here. 'He's eating rocks.'

'That's no rock, *hombre*,' said Ramon, the penguin who'd invited Mumble along. 'It's a *love* stone – for building the nest. The one with the most pebbles wins the heart of the ladies!' He winked.

'So why aren't you collecting pebbles?' asked Mumble curiously.

'Pebbles, schmebbles,' replied the little penguin. 'We got *personality*! Watch and learn, Tall Boy . . .' With that, he and his friends ruffled their crests into impressive hairstyles

50

and whistled at a pair of female penguins coming their way. 'Ju see something ju like, yes?' he said confidently.

'I don't think so,' they replied. 'Not tonight.'

'Oh, don't be so snooty, Booty!' said Ramon.

Eager to keep their female audience interested, the Adelies tried out the new dance steps they'd picked up from Mumble. It worked. 'Where did you learn that?' they asked, fascinated.

'The Big Guy,' said the Adelies. They pointed to Mumble, who blushed.

'Do it again,' said the female penguins.

But the Adelies backed off. 'Sorry, girls,' they said, coyly. 'Some other time, maybe . . .'

The female penguins tutted and walked off, their heads held high.

'Leave 'em wanting more,' Lombardo said. He turned to Mumble and grinned. 'With moves like yours, ju must have all the ladies drooling at your feet!'

'I wouldn't say that,' said Mumble quietly. He could honestly say that *no one* had ever admired his dancing.

Everyone stared.

'Let me tell something to ju,' Ramon said firmly. 'Except for me, Tall Boy, ju got the most charisma of *anybody*.'

'Put that ego away,' groaned the Adelies. 'Your big penguin head is blocking the sun.'

Ramon laughed. 'Oh, you're so jealous,' he said. 'Just a moment . . . I hear people wanting something. Me!'

The little penguins exploded with laughter and, to Mumble's wide-eyed surprise, formed an impromptu conga line. Nothing like this *ever* happened at home. He jumped in behind Ramon and joined the line.

In less time than it took to gobble a fish, Mumble was stepping confidently to the funky beat of the penguins' music. He'd been promoted from the back of the conga line to the front, and the Adelies were doing their level best to keep up with him and all his impromptu moves as he led them through the valley, then up on to the ice ridge. Mumble had *never* had so much fun.

At the very top of the ridge, Mumble twirled around to show the little penguins a flashy move. Suddenly, the icy peak he was balanced

52

on gave way and Mumble dropped right off the edge of the cliff!

'Whooooooo!' he cried as he tobogganed at breakneck speed down an almost vertical slope.

Nestor watched him go. 'Man . . .' he sighed. 'This guy is so accidentally cool.' And he launched himself after Mumble, followed swiftly by the others.

It was the wildest of rides, thrilling and terrifying at the same time. They rocketed down the slope, flung about by the bumps and dips in the ice. First Mumble was in the lead, then the Adelies streaked ahead. *Whoosh!* Mumble slid past, knocking everyone over the edge into an even more terrifying chasm. They zigzagged madly, zooming through tunnels and around curves. It was impossible to steer or slow down.

Meanwhile, the snow that the penguins had knocked from the very tip of the ice mountain was tumbling after them, accelerating and gathering snow and ice as it fell. Soon, it was an avalanche of gigantic proportions, swallowing everything in its path. And it was heading straight for the penguins!

Huge boulders of ice thundered after Mumble and the Adelies, closing in on them, threatening to crush them, when ... the penguins catapulted off a slippery ice ramp and sailed down through the air into the polar sea below. Safely under the blue water, they whooped at the top of their lungs.

Then they realized they were shrouded in darkness.

'I think we broke the ride,' whispered Lombardo.

Way below them, Mumble and the Adelies saw a shaft of light.

'Is that the exit?' asked Ramon gratefully. '*Amigos*,' he said, much cheerier now, 'that was absolutely the best day of my life. So far. Now, all I need is fine foods, fine womens and a super-size siesta –' He broke off, staring goggle-eyed at the Alien creature sitting on the seabed and blocking the exit. 'What ... is ... *that*?' he said slowly.

'Whatever it is, it doesn't belong here,' said Mumble quietly. It was big, and it was rusty. Its massive jaws gaped wide. Mumble headed tentatively towards the motionless monster, swimming all around it, awestruck. Cautiously he tapped the hard body with his beak. At once, the creature came to life. It groaned noisily as it began to sway. A jet of black liquid squirted at Mumble, who ducked and narrowly avoided being bitten by the great jaws. Slowly, the monster broke free from the ice that gripped it and tumbled slowly, end over end, sinking into the dark waters below.

But there was worse to come. The departing creature had set off a deadly chain reaction. The fragile cathedral of ice around them began to disintegrate, walls collapsing all around them in an underwater ice-quake.

Terrified, Mumble and the Adelies swam for their lives.

Chapter 10

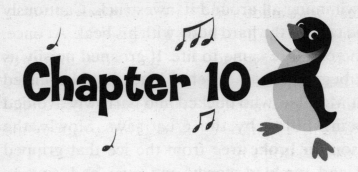

One by one, the Adelies popped out of the sea and scrambled on to solid ice. Mumble torpedoed out of the water, landing safely behind them. Then, without a word, the little penguins sped away.

Mumble hippity-hopped after them. 'Where are we going?' he asked.

'We relocatin',' muttered Nestor, running even faster. 'Placing ourselves elsewhere.'

'But that *thing*!' cried Mumble. 'What was it? Where did it come from?'

'How should we know?' said the Adelies, their heads down. 'We penguins. Very *little* penguins.'

'Hey, guys!' said Mumble. 'We have a mystery here – a mind-boggling mystery!' He stopped dead and made one last plea. '*Amigos!* We've got to get to the bottom of this thing!'

Ramon skidded to a halt and turned to Mumble. The Adelies followed suit and huddled around, listening closely. 'Big guy,' said Ramon. 'Lemme tell something to ju. Come close . . . don't be afraid.'

Mumble leaned forward.

'You want answers?' asked Ramon.

'Yeah,' said Mumble eagerly.

'That's all you need?' said Ramon.

'Yeah,' said Mumble.

'Nothing else?'

'No.'

'Then this is very easy,' said Ramon, looking very pleased with himself. 'You go see Lovelace!'

'Ahhh, Lovelace,' sighed the others. 'Genius, Ramon. You the man!'

Ramon nodded graciously.

This all sounded very encouraging, but Mumble didn't have a clue what they were talking about. 'Who . . . who's Lovelace?' he asked.

'Lovelace is the guru!' explained Lombardo. 'He got the answer to *everything*.'

'But first,' said Ramon, 'ju gonna need a pebble.'

There was a long, long line of penguins stretching across the ice, queuing beside an immense rock tower. Atop the impressive rockpile was a glistening cave, with long, sparkly icicles. Inside the mouth of the cave stood a large, shadowy figure. The mysterious figure stepped forward into the sunlight, revealing a regal Rockhopper penguin with a flamboyant shock of canary-yellow feathers sprouting from his ears and a necklace looped exceedingly tightly around his neck. The plump old penguin stood atop the huge pile of pebbles, surrounded by a gaggle of adoring females.

The first penguin in the queue stepped forward.

'The devotion, please,' said Lovelace, and the penguin added his pebble to the pile. 'And now your question.'

'Señor Lovelace,' the penguin said. 'My wife has disappeared. Is she alive?'

The old Rockhopper turned his back on the crowd, rolled his eyes up into his head and appealed to the heavens. 'Is she alive now?' his deep voice rumbled. 'Speak to me, O Mystic Beings . . .' Lovelace appeared to go into a brief trance, then his body shook and he turned back to the eager penguin. 'Yes!' he cried. 'She is happy and you are in her thoughts.'

'Is she with . . . another male?' asked the penguin.

Lovelace looked stern. 'One pebble – one question,' he said. '*Next!*'

Dejectedly, the penguin hurried away.

The next Adelie bowed and placed a pebble on the pile. 'O Serene One,' he implored. 'Please ask the Mystic Beings . . . will I ever be as rich as you?'

Lovelace looked at his great pile of pebbles and then back at the penguin. 'In your dreams, Gene,' he said. '*Next!*'

Mumble's new friends nudged him forward and, nervously, the fluffy Emperor penguin handed over his pebble. But then up close he could see that the necklace around Lovelace's neck was made of the exact same Alien material as the skua chief's yellow band! The question he'd practised vanished into thin air. 'Have you ever been abducted by Aliens?' he asked instead.

'Excuse me?' croaked Lovelace in astonishment. 'What kind of question is that? *Next!*'

Mumble didn't move. 'I-I met a skua once, with something like that on his foot,' he explained. 'Said he was abducted by Aliens.'

'This, friend,' said Lovelace, touching his necklace reverently, 'is my sacred talisman, bestowed on me by the Mystic Beings during my epic Journey of Enlightenment to the Forbidden Shore.'

His adoring groupies gazed at Lovelace in wonder.

But Mumble wasn't phased. This was most definitely a clue. 'Wait,' he said. 'You saw Mystic Beings?'

'I *hear* them!' Lovelace shouted. 'They speak *through* me!'

Mumble ignored his dramatic cries. He was getting somewhere at last. 'Did they have frontways eyes?' he persisted. 'Did they probe you? Tie you up? Strap you down?'

'Enough!' roared the old Rockhopper. 'That's

too many questions. You don't have enough pebbles, fool.'

'But you haven't answered *any* of my questions,' said Mumble, quite reasonably, he thought.

The queue of penguins was becoming impatient now. 'We've all got stuff to ask, *hombre*!' one heckled. 'Important stuff!' Others joined in, until the noise was deafening.

Lovelace gave a strangled cry. '*Enough!*' He waited until a hush had fallen over the gathering before speaking again. 'You bring this stranger to me,' he said. 'He doubts my powers ... he compares me to a skua! The voices are shrieking in my head. They say: "Lovelace! Who is this fool?"' He took a deep breath and then ran his red eyes over the female penguins clustered around him. 'I will retire now. OK, ladies ... who's first?'

There were shrieks of delight from the groupies, who mobbed the great guru and whisked him behind his pile of pebbles.

The waiting penguins were speechless. 'Hey, wait a minute,' one said. 'What about us?'

All around, penguins began to chant

Lovelace's name, until, rather dishevelled, he reappeared on top of his pebble pile. The crowd fell silent.

'Hear me!' croaked Lovelace. 'There's not enough love in the world! Turn to the penguin next to you . . . and give him a great big hug.' With these words of advice, he vanished once more.

Mumble rolled his eyes and trudged slowly away. He couldn't help feeling that Lovelace was no guru, just a great big fraud who'd tricked the other penguins into giving him a whole heap of pebbles.

'Hey, Stretch!' called Ramon, scurrying after him. 'You got any stones where ju come from?'

'We don't collect stones,' said Mumble dispiritedly. 'We live on the ice.'

'So how ju make a nest and win the heart of the ladies?' asked a puzzled Raul.

'Well . . . we sing,' said Mumble.

The Adelies fell about laughing as if this was the funniest thing they'd ever heard. 'That's crazy!' they said. 'You're kidding, right?'

'No, we sing to each other,' said Mumble

seriously. 'If someone special likes your song, then . . . you know . . .'

Rinaldo swooned. 'And ju have someone *especial*?' he asked. 'A tall beauty in your dark, romantic past, of which ju never speak?'

'Well, sort of,' mumbled Mumble, thinking wistfully of the lovely Gloria.

'Hey, let's go check it out!' piped up Lombardo. 'Maybe she got some friends – I like 'em tall.'

'It's never going to work,' said Mumble sadly.

'Hey, Big Guy, all *ju* gotta do is sing!' said Nestor.

'But that's the problem,' said Mumble, feeling just as stupid as he ever had back in Emperor Land. 'I can't.'

Nestor looked confused. 'Ju a bird, ain't ju?' he said. 'All birds can sing.'

Mumble looked them straight in the eye, opened his beak wide and began to wail. '*FiN*d *ME SOMeBO*dy To*OO* lo*O*vvE!'

'What he doing?' Raul asked the others, who shook their heads. 'That's not singing.'

'Yeah, I heard an animal once do that,' said

Ramon. 'But then they rolled him over . . . he was dead.'

'And when she sings,' said Mumble sadly, 'it darn near breaks your heart.'

The Adelies gave him sympathetic looks, all except Ramon. 'Don't worry,' he said confidently. 'We can fix it.'

'We can?' asked Mumble, his heart lifting.

Ramon beckoned Mumble closer. 'My friend, lemme tell somethin' to ju. Come closer.'

Mumble leaned forward.

'Ju wanna sing?' the little Adelie asked.

'Yeah,' breathed Mumble. 'If I could sing that would change everything!'

'Then this is very easy,' said Ramon. 'Ju will sing. You jus' gotta do exactly what I say . . .'

Chapter 11

Once again, it was mating season in Emperor Land. Single penguins wandered through the crowd, singing their Heartsongs and seeking their soulmates.

One beautiful voice soared above all the rest. But this year, it wasn't Norma Jean. It was Gloria. Tall and elegant, she moved across the ice, her hips swaying as she walked. Male admirers fell over themselves to gain her attention, but she was oblivious . . . until a deep, mesmerizing voice rang out across the ice shelf.

Gloria slowly turned towards the voice. And she was faced with Mumble, singing like an angel – a Spanish angel. As if in a dream, she moved closer, listening curiously to the strange but totally tuneful lyrics.

The Adelies joined Mumble, their flippers slapping to the beat.

'*Mis amigos, este clare, es tire–* Oh hi, Gloria!' Mumble said, interrupting his singing. '*H-hola!*'

'*Hola . . .*' replied Gloria. 'And this is *you*?' she asked.

'Sure it's me,' said Mumble, nervously flashing a big smile. 'You like? *Debe decir, debe gritar . . .*'

'Well, I would,' said Gloria suspiciously, 'if it were really *you*. Yeah.'

Accompanied by the Adelies' cool dance routine, Mumble continued singing, adding quickly, 'It *is* me. Sort of.'

'Yeah,' said Gloria. By now, her tone was distinctly unimpressed. 'Turn around,' she said, trying to take a look behind his back.

In vain, Mumble tried to distract her. '*Lo chegare, sobre salir,*' he sang. 'Why? What's . . .' The song continued, building to an glorious climax. Then, sheepishly, Mumble turned to reveal Ramon, who was doing his very best to be invisible.

'Mumble, how *could* you?' Gloria cried.

'What could you possibly be thinking?'

'I-I didn't know what else to do . . .' said Mumble, hanging his head.

Gloria turned away from Mumble in disbelief as she walked towards the cluster of all her many male admirers, each one crooning a charming melody. Half-heartedly, she joined in, singing her own beautiful tune. But the hurt in her voice was unmistakable.

Mumble couldn't bear it. There *had* to be something he could do. There had to be some way of making up for the trick he'd played, some way to win Gloria's respect. Then he had an idea.

'Gloria,' he said desperately. 'Sing to this . . .' He tapped his flippers loudly on the ice. *Tip-tap-tippity-tippity-tap,* in rhythm with Gloria's song.

'Mumble, you're embarrassing me,' said Gloria, going on with her Heartsong.

Mumble leaped on to a mound of ice and tried again, louder this time. *TAP-TIPPITY-TAP-TAP.* His moves and rhythm were so undeniably catchy that, very slowly, Gloria began to warm to the beat – a beat that felt inexplicably connected to the spirit of her own. And, gaining in confidence, Mumble danced like never before. *Tip-tap-tippity-tippity-tap tap-tippity tap!* Totally won over now, Gloria sang from the bottom of her heart.

Then a very strange thing happened. Mumble's dancing and Gloria's singing began to merge together as one. Gloria's feet starting tap-tippity-tapping too. Together, they made quite a pair.

The irresistible rhythm of the song-and-dance routine was infectious, and soon the other penguins began to dance. Some followed Mumble's lead, while others took up Gloria's song. Happy feet were spreading like wildfire. The youngsters joined in, chanting in time to the beat. The Adelies joined in. Even Miss Viola joined in. It was the most wonderful moment of Mumble's entire life.

The sound and music carried even further afield, catching Maurice's attention. 'Hey,' he said to Memphis, peering into the distance. 'It's your boy!'

Norma Jean overheard. 'Mumble?' she said.

'Mumble!' cried Memphis.

But not everyone was as entranced by the new craze. A group of Elders watched disapprovingly from their lofty perch as the commotion grew. And, just when it seemed as if the Penguin Nation might abandon itself entirely to the dancing, Eggbert the Elder spoke.

'This was an omen from the start,' he said angrily, fixing Noah with an accusatory look. 'And now we have this . . . uprising!'

Noah surveyed the dancing crowds below, narrowing his eyes. Mumble had already managed to rally the younger penguin community to his preposterous dancing! With the fish shortage at hand, Emperor Land was falling on hard times, and everything he had worked for was now held together by a mere thread. *'Stop!'* he roared. *'Stop this unruly nonsense!'*

Chapter 12

It was enough to put the dampers on any party. The fun petered out . . . and swiftly died.

Mumble was the very last to come to a standstill. He looked up at the Elders in dismay.

'You dare to bring this disorder to the very heart of our community?' Noah said. 'Have you lost your minds?'

'We're just having fun,' protested one of the younger penguins. 'Harmless fun . . .'

'Harmless?' cried Noah. 'It is this kind of backsliding that has brought the Scarcity upon us!'

Lombardo stepped forward. 'Excuse me, Smiley,' he said. 'Can ju speak plain penguin, please?'

'He thinks the food shortage has something

70

to do with me,' Mumble muttered under his breath.

Noah the Elder addressed Mumble angrily. 'Do you not understand that we can only survive here when we are in harmony?' he said. 'When you and your foreign friends lead us into your easy ways, you offend the Great Guin. You invite him to withhold his bounty!'

Mumble looked around uneasily. He knew that a battle was underway – a battle for the hearts and minds of the gathered crowd. 'Wait a minute!' he protested. 'Happy feet can't cause a famine!'

Eggbert the Elder joined in. 'If this kind of unruly display did not cause it, then what did?'

Mumble took his time in replying. He thought about the skua's bracelet and Lovelace's necklace and the strange material they were both made of. 'I think it comes from outside,' he said carefully. 'Way beyond the ice. There are things out there we don't understand.'

'Mysteries . . .' said the Adelies. 'Mind-boggling mysteries . . . Mystic Beings!'

'Yeah,' agreed Mumble. 'Aliens!'

'He's mad,' said the Elders, shaking their heads. 'Insane.'

'No!' shouted Mumble. He *had* to make them listen. 'They might be smarter than *all* of us.'

Eggbert wasn't having any of it. 'He drove the fish away and now he's ranting this rubbish!' he shouted to the crowd.

But the Adelies jumped to Mumble's defence. 'Hey, let me tell something to ju!' shouted Ramon, waddling right up to the Elders.

'Don't touch me, you little wretch!' shouted Eggbert, batting the little penguin aside with a flipper. This was too much for the Adelies, and a scuffle broke out between them and the Elders. Mumble desperately tried to break it up.

'And so it follows,' Noah boomed ominously. 'Dissent leads to division, and division leads us to doom. You, Mumble Happy Feet, must go!'

Mumble was shocked. But then a familiar figure rushed from the crowd and flung her flipper around him. It was his mother. 'Don't you take one step, sweetheart,' she said. 'You have as much right to be here as any of these daffy old fools!'

'Norma Jean!' Memphis suddenly appeared, towering over them both. 'I'll deal with this,' he announced. He looked from Noah and the Elders to his son.

Mumble felt a small surge of hope and pride. Finally, his father was going to stand by him.

'Mumble.' Memphis turned to his son, his voice deep and serious. 'You must renounce your so-called friends, your peculiar thoughts and your . . . your strange ways . . .'

'Memphis!' cried Norma Jean, horrified.

'. . . If we are devout and sincere in our praise,' Memphis continued, 'the fish will return.'

'They *will*,' said Eggbert. The other Elders murmured their agreement.

'But, Pa!' Mumble protested. He was completely stunned.

'Listen, boy,' said Memphis gently, 'I was a backslider myself. I was careless, and now we're paying the price.'

'What's this got to do with Mumble?' asked Norma Jean, clearly taken aback.

'It's why he is the way he is,' said Memphis.

'But there's nothing *wrong* with him,' she protested.

'Face it, Norma Jean . . . our son is all messed up!'

'Our son is *not* messed up, you hear me?' she exclaimed.

'Believe me, I know he is!' said Memphis, finally exasperated.

'*How* can you say that?' said Norma Jean angrily.

'Because –' Memphis paused in agony, his face a picture of guilt – 'when he was just an egg, I *dropped* him!'

The crowd gasped and fell silent.

'Oh, Memphis!' cried Norma Jean. 'Oh, my poor little Mumble!'

Mumble couldn't see what all the fuss was about. 'Ma, I'm perfectly fine,' he insisted.

'No you're not, boy,' said Memphis. 'For all our sakes, you must stop with this freakiness with the feet.'

'Your father speaks wisely,' said Noah the Elder.

Mumble ignored him. 'But it just doesn't

make any sense,' he said, his eyes pleading with Memphis to listen. 'Don't ask me to change, Pa . . . because I can't.'

Memphis hung his head and made no reply.

'Your arrogance leaves us no choice,' concluded Noah. He pointed at Mumble. 'You, *begone*!'

'Mumble . . .' wailed his mother, her eyes welling with tears.

'Ma, it's OK,' Mumble replied. He felt strangely numb. How had it come to this? His father thought that there was something wrong with him. The Elders thought that he was the reason for the fish shortage. Mumble squared his shoulders and faced Noah. 'Let me tell something to *you*,' he said. 'When I find out what's happening to the fish, I'll be back.' As he turned to leave, the crowd parted to let him pass.

Proudly, he hippity-hopped through the penguin colony, followed by a dignified procession of Adelies.

'Together we prevail,' Noah said quietly, turning towards the community.

'In the Wisdoms we trust,' responded the colony, including Memphis.

Norma Jean looked at her mate in disbelief.

But one voice rang out over the crowd. 'Mumble, you don't have to go!' cried Gloria. 'This isn't fair!'

But Mumble kept walking. He was determined to discover the truth and would not come back until he found it.

The egg performed a neat backflip, before landing on its feet and lurching off across the ice.

'I wouldn't do that around here, son,' Memphis said quietly.

'As long as all three of us are together, everything's gonna be just fine.'

'A penguin without a Heartsong is hardly a penguin at all.'

Now they could see how easy it was, the rest of the penguins followed suit.

'What's wrong with you?' shouted a penguin.

'That's not singing!' Raul shook his head.

'Who is this fool?'

Gloria slowly turned towards the voice.

'Face it, Norma Jean . . . our son is messed up!'

'How could we keep an egg safe?' Mumble asked Gloria.

In one single day Mumble had managed
to lose everything.

Lovelace struggled for breath as the necklace held
tight around his neck.

It was a dreadful place, this Alien world.

'*Adios, amigos!* I'm going to find out what's happening to our fish,' Mumble took a few paces back.

There were an awful lot of Happy Feet.

Chapter 13

'Don't worry, Tall Guy,' said Ramon. 'My father also call me a pitiful loser . . . look how I turn out!'

'Ju not helping, Ramon,' muttered Nestor.

Mumble plodded on, lost in thought.

'He going to be OK,' Rinaldo said brightly. 'All he got to do is find out what happen to the fish.'

'The Aliens!' announced Mumble suddenly. 'I'm going to talk to the Aliens.'

'*How* you going to find Aliens?' asked Lombardo.

'Lovelace,' Mumble replied.

'But he don't like ju,' Raul pointed out.

'That's OK,' said Mumble. He wasn't going to let a little thing like that stand in his way.

After all, not many people seemed to like him in Emperor Land either. 'I'll appeal to his better nature,' he said.

When they arrived, the rock tower was completely deserted, and Lovelace was nowhere to be seen. Finally, they found him, sprawled out behind his pile of pebbles.

'Lovelace?' called Nestor softly, tiptoeing forward. 'I-I know we don't have an appointment, but –'

'Just one question – and I want a straight answer,' interrupted Mumble, who wasn't in the mood for pleasantries. He ignored the Adelies' horrified looks. 'Where do I find the Mystic Beings?' There was no answer, so Mumble aimed a deft kick at the pile of pebbles, which sprayed everywhere.

'Why don't he speak?' asked Nestor. 'Lovelace, ju OK?'

There was a tight, low gurgling from Lovelace's throat.

'Aye! He's possessed!' Nestor cried.

'A seizure!' yelled Rinaldo. 'Open the beak! Grab his tongue!'

Wincing and gasping, his eyes bulging as if they might pop, Lovelace pointed to the necklace. Suddenly, Mumble guessed what was really wrong and realized why the old penguin had always had such a croaky way of speaking. 'He's choking!' he said. 'That thing around his neck . . . it's way too tight!'

'Well, why didn't you say so?' said Raul. 'Come on . . . on three!' Each of the Adelies grabbed a piece of the necklace with their beak. '*Uno . . . dos . . . tres . . . cuatro!*' they counted, and pulled. Hard.

'Stop!' Mumble pleaded. '*Amigos!* You're hurting him!'

Guiltily, the Adelies stopped tugging.

'Any better?' said Ramon.

Lovelace wiggled his flipper from side to side, as if to say that he wasn't so bad.

'How did you get that thing around your neck?' asked Mumble. He was determined now to get to the bottom of this. 'Did the Mystic Beings bestow it on you?'

The Rockhopper shook his head sadly.

'He don't know what he sayin'!' protested Ramon.

Lovelace, who was still too shaken up to speak, motioned with his flippers.

Mumble translated. 'You were swimming and it just got caught around your neck?' he asked. The plump old penguin gurgled and nodded. 'Did you ever actually meet a Mystic Being?' said Mumble. 'Officially?'

Lovelace gasped and shook his head again.

'No way!' protested the Adelies. 'He the guru!'

A tear slid down Lovelace's beak.

'I knew it!' announced Rinaldo, swiftly changing tack. 'It's all a lie!'

Mumble examined the necklace. 'But this belongs to *someone*,' he said thoughtfully. 'And if we could find *them*, I bet they could take it off.'

The old penguin looked up, a glimmer of hope in his eye.

'Show me where you found it,' said Mumble, kinder now. 'I'm sure they could help us – you and me both.'

Lovelace gestured and croaked eagerly, making a strange 'Oi, oi, oi' sound.

'Two words, three syllables?' guessed the Adelies. They guffawed. 'Ay yai yai. Now he thinks he's an Elephant seal!'

To everyone's surprise, the Rockhopper nodded. Then he pointed to the mountains.

'Go over the mountains?' said Lombardo.

Lovelace nodded again.

'To the land of the Elephant seals?'

At this, Lovelace looked really excited. He gestured wildly with his flippers.

'Ahhh,' said Mumble. He was getting the hang of this game. '*Beyond* the land of the Elephant seals . . .'

Lovelace gave a final emphatic nod and fell back in exhaustion.

'Yay!' cried the Adelies.

But, at that moment, Mumble was thinking very hard, hope rising in his heart. If they found the beings who could take off the rings for Lovelace, then maybe they could discover once and for all what had happened to all the fish.

Chapter 14

The weary band of intrepid penguins came to a halt. A hostile landscape stretched before them – a vast field of ice carved by the wind into massive ridges. A cold wind blew, and with it came the distant but unmistakable sound of a . . . *voice*.

Mumble and the Adelies looked curiously all around. There was no one. And yet, there it was again.

'Mumble!'

A lone figure appeared over the ridge behind them. Mumble squinted. It was an Emperor penguin, but from this distance he couldn't tell who it was.

'*Mumble Happy Feet!*' cried the voice, louder now.

Mumble couldn't believe his eyes. 'Gloria?' he murmured. Then, at the top of his voice, '*Gloria!*' She'd been following their trail since he'd left Emperor Land, and had caught them up at last. 'W-what are you doing here?' he asked, stunned.

In reply, Gloria sang him the most wonderful tune. 'Which way, Twinkle Toes?' she said afterwards, her eyes sparkling.

'Oh my,' sighed Mumble, clearly overwhelmed by the knowledge that Gloria, the most sought-after penguin in Emperor Land, had come after him. For a moment, he felt almost giddy with happiness. But then the reality hit him like a block of ice. He could not let Gloria do this. He could not let her follow him into uncertainty, into danger. 'Oh . . . no, no, no,' he said. 'I-if you come, you may never get back home.'

'Fine by me,' said Gloria briskly.

'You have a life back there,' said Mumble slowly. 'I don't. I mean . . . *we* don't. Not out here.' He was babbling now. 'How could we keep an egg safe? That's if we ever had an egg . . .'

'Well, I don't need an egg to be happy,' said Gloria.

It's not working! he thought quickly and tried again. 'Well, y-you say that now,' he said. 'But what about later, when all your friends have eggs?'

'Then I'll have you,' Gloria said.

I've got to get her back to Emperor Land, he told himself firmly. *Even if it means . . . losing her.*

But the Adelies looked highly delighted with the developing situation. 'Ahhhhh . . .' they sighed, whispering amongst themselves. 'Now he going to pledge his soul forever. Here it comes . . .'

'Gloria,' said Mumble. 'I'm a particular kind of guy – the kind of guy who . . . needs his own space.'

'Huh?' whispered the Adelies.

'Oh,' said Gloria, looking as if she didn't believe him one bit.

'It's not you . . . it's me,' said Mumble, trying to sound aloof. 'I'm just not up for a serious relationship right now.'

'What he's trying to do now,' Ramon translated, 'is push her away.'

'No matter what you say or do,' said Gloria,

'you're stuck with me. Oh, come on. As if you're not totally thrilled that I'm here!'

'Now she got him on the ropes,' said Ramon, looking excitedly from one Emperor penguin to the other.

'Here's your problem,' provoked Mumble. 'You think you're irresistible, don't you?'

Gloria looked shaken. 'Excuse me?' she said.

'Gloria's so gorgeous,' Mumble mimicked. 'Gloria's so talented.' Then he said the one thing that he knew would push her away forever. 'Just because you can hit a few high notes.'

The Adelies gasped.

'You got a problem with my singing?' asked Gloria, wounded.

'It's perfectly . . . fine,' said Mumble.

'Ooooh,' said Ramon.

'If you like that sort of thing,' added Mumble. 'It's a little nana-tootsie for my taste. You know, showy . . . flashy . . . frou-frou.'

'Ouch.' Ramon winced.

'Frou-frou?' gasped Gloria. She was shocked. She could barely believe what she was hearing.

'That's right,' said Mumble, ploughing forward, knowing the damage had been done.

Gloria pulled herself together – the hurt in her eyes turning quickly to anger. 'Hah!' she said, livid. 'And this comes from someone who thinks it's cool to jig up and down really fast on the spot . . . like some twitchy *idiot*!'

Mumble wanted nothing more than to impress Gloria. Instead he rudely burst into a frenzy of tapping. 'What'd you say? I couldn't hear you over all the tapping!' he yelled out, ending in an incredible triple pirouette, just millimetres from Gloria's angry face.

'Egghh!' she cried. 'You stubborn, hippity-hoppity *fool*!'

Mumble's reply was even more wild tapping.

Gloria gave a great cry of anger and frustration, turned on her heel and started on the long journey back home.

Sadly, Mumble watched her go. He didn't belong in Emperor Land. He knew he'd done the right thing. He couldn't just stand by and watch Gloria being made an outcast too, but that still didn't make him feel any better. How had he managed to lose everything in one single day? His chance to find acceptance at home, his family and now . . . Gloria.

'Come on, guys. Let's keep going.' He sighed, feeling more depressed than ever.

The Adelies clustered round him as the journey resumed.

'*Amigo*, that was a good thing ju do,' said Nestor.

'She is going to be so much better without ju,' added Ramon. 'She is going to find a good steady guy to comfort her *real* good and raise a big family . . .'

'Shhhh!' said Raul.

'. . . and then she's going to let herself go and –'

'Ramon!' snapped Rinaldo. 'He's hurting *bad*.'

'Oooh.' But the irrepressible Ramon couldn't be quiet for long. 'Listen . . . Don't hold it in, or ju esplode,' he told Mumble. 'You got to let it out!'

Mumble trudged onwards, his feet slapping lightly on the ice. He'd done it now. Gloria would *never* be his. And she'd never know how much he really loved her.

Chapter 15

Mile after mile the penguins marched onward towards the distant land of the Elephant seals. Lovelace was having trouble breathing, and every step made him wheeze and gurgle all the more. As they plodded up yet another frozen ridge, Mumble stopped to check on the old Rockhopper. 'Can you keep going?' he asked, concerned.

But before Lovelace could reply, a strange roar echoed across the icy wasteland.

'Oi! Oi! Oi! Oi!'

The Adelies had heard it too. 'Hey, Fluffy!' called Ramon from the top of the ridge. 'We're following ju – get up here!'

Mumble didn't need to be asked twice. He ran, slipping and sliding to the Adelies' vantage point, dragging Lovelace with him. And there it was at last – the land of the Elephant seals. The sound they'd heard was the 'Oi, oi, oi' of thousands of seals.

'So . . . er . . . these Elephant seals . . .' began Lombardo. 'They're not penguin-eaters, are they?'

'I *believe* they are herbivores,' said Ramon, not sounding entirely convinced. 'Ju know, kelp-suckers?'

'Here we go, Lovelace!' announced Mumble, as he pushed him down the hill. 'Down is *easy*.' Hope welling inside him, they slip-slided towards the seals.

Reluctantly, the Adelies followed. The penguins whizzed down the icy slope, landing right in front of two great, big-bellied monsters.

'You boys better be lost,' boomed the larger of the two. 'Because trespassing's a – *burp!* – crime.'

'A criminal crime,' added the second seal. 'Carrying a penalty of enormous – *BURP!* – weight.'

Trying not to laugh at the Elephant seals' constant belching, Mumble pointed into the distance. 'Ah . . . we're just passing through,' he said.

'Wait,' said the first seal incredulously. 'You squirts ain't heading over them there distant hills?'

Mumble gulped. The seals weren't exactly being encouraging. 'If that's the only way to the Forbidden Shore,' he said.

Slowly, and with much slurping, the first seal sucked his great snout into his mouth and spat it out. '*Phhlurrr!* The Forbidden Shore?' he snorted.

The two seals chortled nastily.

'Well, be our guest,' said the bigger seal. 'You might come face to face with an *Annihilator*.'

Mumble's mind whirred. 'An *Alien* Annihilator?' he asked curiously.

'They're the ones,' exclaimed the seals. 'Cut you up as soon as look at you. Annihilate *every living thing* in their path.'

Mumble thought quickly. Were the Annihilators and the Mystic Beings the same creatures? 'Could they be annihilating fish?' he asked.

'Could be,' said the first seal, burping again loudly. 'I heard they'd take a whole whale and turn it into mush.'

Not to be outdone, the second seal added, '*I* heard they'd take that mush, twirl it around their head, stomp it on the ground and suck it through a straw!'

For a moment, Mumble was speechless. He didn't think much of the Elephant seals, but still . . . what sort of animal would *do* such a thing to its fellow creatures? And if they did this to mighty whales, what chance was there for the fish? Then Mumble remembered: the skua had appealed to their better nature. They must have one . . . there might still be hope.

'I'm too pretty to die!' moaned Ramon.

'Did you actually see these Aliens yourself?' Mumble asked the seals.

They sucked in their snouts and spat them out in disgust. 'Who in their right mind would *want* to?' they barked.

Lovelace, who had been struggling for breath, choked noisily.

Mumble gave Lovelace a worried look. They'd better hurry, or it might be too late for the wheezy old Rockhopper. 'Come on,' he said. 'Let's go.' Together, he and Lovelace set off towards the mountains.

For the first time, the Adelies hesitated. They were fearful of what they had learned from the Elephant seals and were unsure about the danger that lay before them. Unwillingly, the Adelies tagged along behind – afraid of the journey ahead, but, in the end, too afraid to go back on their own.

A few soft snowflakes drifted from a leaden sky. With dizzying speed, the snowflakes multiplied to become a terrible snowstorm. Slowly, Mumble led a sombre conga of penguins through the driving snow and ice. It was tough going. 'I'm getting cold feet about this . . .' moaned Raul.

Rinaldo agreed. 'Even my cold feet are getting cold feet,' he said.

A sudden, extra-harsh gust of wind knocked Lovelace down and blew the Adelies out of sight. Mumble stopped and scooped up the old Rockhopper, then tried to push on. But the gale was so fierce that he couldn't take a step . . . until, out of the blizzard, came the plucky

Adelies, marching in time. They gathered behind Mumble and Lovelace and propelled them forward through the snow.

After trekking for hours, the penguins reached a rocky cave where they could take shelter from the storm. Sometime during the night, the blizzard died away, leaving behind an eerie stillness.

Mumble awoke with a start. 'What's that noise?' he demanded.

'There *is* no noise,' said Rinaldo.

'No gasping, no wheezing?' asked Raul.

Lovelace was gone.

'Sometimes, a brave penguin will just slip away to die,' said Nestor dramatically.

'Do ju think he went to a happy place?' Lombardo mused.

'No, no!' said Mumble, pointing to tracks that led out of the shelter across the fresh snow. 'I think he went *this* way.' He followed the tracks out into the daylight. They led towards a group of strange buildings.

'The Forbidden Shore . . .' he breathed. They had reached it at last.

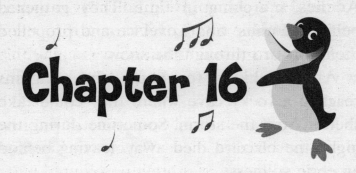

Chapter 16

The penguins ventured forward, tracking Lovelace's snowy footprints. It was a dreadful place, this Alien world. The old, decrepit buildings towered over them. They were filled with evil-looking metal objects, festooned with icicles or half covered by snow. Mumble shuddered. Was this the place where the Aliens did unspeakable things to whales?

'Lovelace!' he shouted, more desperate now.

There was no reply.

Mumble went on, the Adelies close behind.

'Hmm . . . his feets don't look too good,' said Raul, looking at the snow. Then he pointed at a scuffed hollow. 'He rested here!' The tracks told their own bleak story. Lovelace had fallen on to his belly, then his behind. He'd got up. He'd fallen over again.

The Adelies wove back and forth, their beaks to the ground. 'Then he was going this way . . . No, this way . . . Over there . . . There he goes . . .'

Mumble was the only penguin tall enough to spot Lovelace up ahead. The old Rockhopper had collapsed against a brightly coloured buoy at the edge of the ice. 'There he is!' he cried. 'Lovelace, we're here!'

Lovelace looked up wearily and pointed with effort towards the water, which was lapping against the ice. Mumble couldn't help but notice that the pauses between each of his laboured breaths were getting longer.

There, floating on the water, were an old boot, a rope, a can . . . and a necklace just like the one that the Rockhopper wore, made of the same Alien material. 'Look! There's one for everyone,' said Raul.

'Just hang in there,' Mumble said to Lovelace, scanning all around. 'I know they're here somewhere.'

'Yeah,' agreed Ramon. 'They wouldn't leave all this behind.'

'Maybe they're invisible?' suggested Rinaldo.

They all reached out nervously and were feeling cautiously for invisible beings when . . . Lovelace stopped breathing.

Frantically, Mumble and the Adelies were trying to revive the old bird, when the bell on the buoy tolled loudly, as if warning them.

'Please!' cried Mumble, to anyone who would listen. 'We need some help here!'

Behind them, an ominous wave rose out of the glassy surface of the sea. A huge shadow fell over them. But it wasn't the help they were hoping for. They spun round to see a huge orca towering above, its black and white skin glistening with water.

Crash! A second orca smashed through the peninsula on which the penguins stood, instantly cutting them off. Helplessly, they floated adrift on a spinning chunk of ice.

Suddenly, Lovelace gasped and sat up.

'He's back!' cried Ramon. 'All he needed was fresh air.'

'So where we going?' asked Raul.

'A sea cruise!' said Lombardo hopefully.

Mumble watched as the orcas circled, nudging

the ice plate, which lurched from side to side and made the bell chime non-stop. Slowly but surely, they were heading out to sea.

'Whatever you do, stay out of the water!' warned Mumble.

But the weakened Lovelace just couldn't hang on. He slipped off the ice into the water, dragging the bell with him. Desperately, everyone rushed to the other side of the ice plate, but the bell pinged upright again. Lovelace was out of the water, but was now dangling from the top of the bell, caught by his necklace! An orca rose from the water and eyed the Rockhopper's plump bottom – a particularly tasty snack!

'Kick him, Lovelace!' called Mumble. But the bell broke away from the buoy, and Mumble stared in horror as the Rockhopper plummeted into the water, dragged down by the bell. Immediately Mumble jumped in after him – his only thought was to save Lovelace from the depths below.

Seconds later, the poor Adelies were flicked from the ice plate by a huge tail. They leaped desperately on to a very small and unstable chunk of ice, watching in horror as an orca surged out of the water. Dangling from its mouth were Mumble, Lovelace and the bell.

The massive orca flung his prizes high. They whistled through the air in a gentle arc before landing right in front of another orca. Back and forth Mumble and Lovelace went, in a cruel game of catch.

The Adelies stared. 'If they're the appetizers,' said Lombardo miserably, 'we're the main course.'

'I don't think any of us is *really* a main meal,' commented Nestor.

'We're more like tapas,' Raul said.

'Is this helping to reconcile you to your imminent death?' asked Ramon casually.

'No!' cried the other Adelies.

Suddenly, something wonderful happened. *Snap!* All the whizzing to and fro had pulled Lovelace free of his necklace. He whooped with joy, able to breath and speak and – surprisingly – rhyme.

'Rejoice, rejoice, I found my voice!' cried the Rockhopper. 'Been a cheater, been a liar, my purpose now will be much higher . . .'

'Reach out to me!' shouted Mumble, wondering if, perhaps, he'd liked Lovelace better when he was a little quieter. They collided in mid-air, clutching each other in a big, desperate hug, before plunging into the ocean.

Now the orcas turned their attention to the trembling Adelies, tossing them off the ice into the sea. They swam for their lives, their pursuers close behind. Just in time, the little penguins made it to shore, followed closely by the orcas.

Peeoww! Mumble and Lovelace followed, torpedoing out of the water, sailing over the heads of the surprised orcas and landing neatly by the Adelies.

Lovelace puffed up to his full height, ready for the showdown at hand. 'This is a bad day for you, my friends!' he bellowed, with not a trace of a croak. 'You dealing with Lovelace now. You flaccid-finned overblown baitfish! You turn round right now! Hightail it back to your mommas!'

And, without so much as a murmur, the orcas obeyed. They turned around and swam silently away into a rising fog.

The Adelies cheered. They couldn't believe their luck.

But Mumble was utterly shocked. 'Why did they do that?' he murmured. 'They could have eaten us all in one bite.'

Chapter 17

'How did you *do* that?' asked Raul, impressed.

'I am Lovelace!' boomed the Rockhopper. 'I draw my power from a deep well of courage –'

Suddenly, there was an earth-shattering noise and a colossal black shape loomed out of the fog. No wonder the orcas had hightailed it! The pack ice churned and buckled into the air, exploding in front of the mighty vessel before it slid smoothly by.

'Come on, Fluffy, ju know they don't want to chit-chat,' Ramon said quickly.

'I think they want to be alone,' said Rinaldo.

'And we should respect that,' added Nestor.

'But this is what we came for,' Mumble insisted. 'Come on!' he said, hardly noticing that, pushed by the great ship, the ice was rising upwards. They raced to the highest point on the glacier and watched, transfixed, as the fog cleared and the black monster joined a crowd of identical vessels.

'What are they doing here?' asked Mumble in awe. 'It's like they don't even know we exist.'

'Let me tell something to ju,' Ramon said sternly. 'This is the end of the road. Is over. Ju did everything penguinly possible.'

'Ju found the Aliens,' said Nestor.

'We're going to testify to that,' added Lovelace.

'We tell your whole laughing-boy nation they were dead wrong about ju,' said Lombardo. 'Now, let's get back home, right now!'

Mumble listened to his friends. He could hear it in their voices that they all wanted to go back. He recognized the great danger that lay ahead, but he himself hadn't come this far to give up now. He *had* to find the fish. He was determined to keep the promise he had made back in Emperor Land. 'Could I ask a favour of you?' he said to the Adelies.

'Sure,' they replied, happy to be going home.

'Could you make sure Gloria's OK? And my ma? And, if you see Pa . . . tell him I tried.'

'What ju talking about?' demanded Rinaldo.

'I'm going to go find out what's happening to our fish,' Mumble said, taking a few paces back.

'No!' cried the other penguins in alarm. 'What are ju doing?'

In reply, Mumble hippity-hopped forward, going faster and faster until he charged right over the edge of the iceberg into space. '*Adios, amigos!*' he cried, diving into the sea.

'*Madre mia!*' Nestor exclaimed. The penguins ran to the edge, horrified.

'No penguin could make it through that fall!' The Adelies watched, completely shocked.

'Look! He's swimmin'!' shouted Ramon, pointing. Mumble surfaced, far away against the lapping waves, swimming in the direction of the big black ships. Ramon shook his head, awestruck. 'How tall ju think that Tall Boy was?'

'Taller than anyone . . .' replied Lovelace. 'You're gonna be a legend, Happy Feet, a tale told for all time!'

But Mumble could not hear his friends calling out to him. As he swam against the powerful waves, he only had one thought running through his mind: to find out what had happened to the fish. Finally, as he neared the Alien ship, he saw a huge net teeming with ... FISH – thousands of them! And it was rising slowly, up through the water to the side of the Alien vessel. In that moment, Mumble understood – it was the Aliens who were taking the fish! *Never* in his life had he imagined that they would be the source of the food shortage. And, for the first time in his life, Mumble was filled with a deep, overpowering sense of anger.

'Hey!' Mumble yelled, furiously. 'You're taking our fish! Wait! Hey! *Stop!*' He grabbed hold of the net with his teeth and was carried up with it, out of the water and towards the ship. A mysterious figure prised Mumble away from the net with a pole, but Mumble was determined to hang on. Then another poked him, and still another, sending him plummeting back into the sea at last. Then the engines started up again, churning the waters around him.

Millions of bubbles blinded him, and when

the foamy sea finally stopped stirring around Mumble, the ships were far away on the horizon.

Mumble swam after the black ships for a very long time, relentlessly surfing mountainous waves and the treacherous waters. But the ships sailed further and further into the distance, eventually vanishing to where the sea met the sky. Swept by the currents, the brave penguin persevered north, away from his icy home.

Wave after wave crashed over him, and still he went on and on, until, one dreadful night, Mumble became so tired that it was like swimming through treacle. His limbs felt too heavy to move – he could go no further. As if in a dream, he saw a strange shore . . . horrible stickiness . . . bright lights . . . and he finally gave in to blackness.

Chapter 18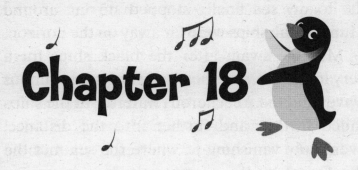

Mumble opened his eyes and blinked in amazement. He was inside a tunnel and up ahead was a bright, shining light. He walked towards it as if in a trance. He didn't know where he was, but outwardly it looked like home. There was snow and bright blue sky and there were white cliffs of ice. And all around, there were penguins of all different kinds.

'Excuse me . . .' he said to no one in particular. 'What is this place?'

A plump Chinstrap penguin waddled by in a zombie-like trance. 'You're in heaven, friend,' he said. 'Penguin heaven.'

'Is it anywhere near Emperor Land?' Mumble asked.

'It's wherever you want it to be . . .' said the dazed-looking penguin.

Mumble headed towards a distant ice shelf. *Bang!* He had walloped straight into a wall. He dizzily reeled back and realized that the ice shelf wasn't an ice shelf at all. It was all fake!

'Try the water, friend,' suggested the zombie friend. 'It's really real.'

Mumble stumbled back into the water and looked around at his strange new environment. And there, under the water and behind a thick wall of reflected glass, were the Aliens! They looked like big, ugly penguins with fat, flabby faces, frontways eyes and the strangest appendages, just as the skua had said.

At long last, Mumble was going to find out what was going on! 'Excuse me,' he said politely. 'Why are you taking our fish? We can't survive without them!'

But the Aliens just walked away without answering.

'No, wait!' cried Mumble. He shot to the surface and landed on the ice. To his surprise, he could see many more Aliens in the galleries above and all around.

'Oh . . . oh my!' said Mumble brightly, amazed at the size of his audience. Surely someone would be able to help him here. 'Ah, hello! Hello from Emperor Land! I'm sure you don't mean to, but you're causing an awful lot of grief!'

No one replied. They all just stared at him.

'Don't you understand?' Mumble shouted. 'I'm speaking plain Penguin! You're stealing our fish! You're kind of killing us out there! TALK TO ME!'

But all that the Aliens saw was a squawking penguin in the zoo. Every day, torrents of fish rained into his glass prison. After three days, Mumble lost his voice. And after three weeks he almost lost his mind. He had spent all his energy hurling himself against the glass wall in increasingly frantic attempts to communicate with the Aliens, but to no avail.

While the Aliens came day after day to stare at him, all Mumble could see was visions of those he loved most in his life, hungry and wasting away. There were his mother and Gloria, with Memphis to one side, his head turned away from Mumble. The Adelies were there too, asking how long it would be until he was back. He tried to share his wealth of fish with the apparitions of his loved ones, but it was no use. He was flinging the fish, one after the other, against a wall.

And Mumble's story would have ended right there if it had not been for . . .

Tap tap tap.

A little Alien – a girl – was tapping on the glass, trying to get his attention.

It took a while for the sound to filter into Mumble's scrambled mind, but eventually he looked up. Slowly, his foot responded. *Tap tap tap.*

And the little girl replied back: *Tap tap tap.*

Something awakened inside Mumble and a half-remembered rhythm came back to him. *Tap-tap-tappity-tippity-tap.*

Grinning widely, the girl answered Mumble's rhythm on the glass. *Tap-tap-tappity-tippity-tap.*

Just as he had when Gloria had tapped his egg, Mumble felt as if he was coming alive, the familiar sounds of his Heartsong bringing new life to his body. *Tap-tap-tappity-tippity-tappity-tap-tap-tap*. His feet were moving faster now.

The little girl burst out laughing. She took her mother by the hand and pulled her over to the glass to see. The mother stared in disbelief.

Soon a crowd of humans gathered, laughing, clapping and beaming with delight.

Mumble's heart soared. After weeks of trying, he had *finally* found a way to get through to them!

'Trust me. You won't believe your eyes!' said an excited Alien.

'He's *communicating* with us!' said another. 'We tap – he answers! Where on earth did you find this creature?'

'He washed up on a beach, all the way from South Antarctica!' answered another Alien, nodding.

Chapter 19

Back in Emperor Land, the penguins were weak from lack of food. They were listless, subdued and very hungry. Such a sense of hopelessness was in the air that no one noticed the tiny figure hippity-hopping purposefully across the vast icy landscape towards them.

'Hey!' cried the lone figure, as he approached the penguins. 'Hello!'

At first, all the penguins didn't recognize the sleek and well-fed penguin in front of them.

'Isn't that the fellow with the wacky feet?' said one penguin, staring into the distance. 'What was his name?'

Others gathered curiously to watch. 'I thought he was dead,' said another penguin.

Mumble clambered on to an icy rise and

called out excitedly, 'Hey, everybody! Listen up! I've got big news! I know who's taking the fish – it's the Aliens! I made contact with them!'

The gathering crowd muttered suspiciously.

'I think they want to help us!' cried Mumble.

Suddenly, an elegant female penguin stepped forward. 'Hey, you!' she said.

'Gloria!' exclaimed Mumble, noticing the dozen fluffy chicks all gathered at her feet. There was a sudden lump in his throat as he found himself realizing that his chance with her was gone.

'You're looking different,' she said. 'Kind of *flashy*.'

A larger penguin pushed through the crowd. 'Everything cool here, baby?' he asked.

'You remember Seymour,' said Gloria.

Mumble nodded. 'Oh, yeah,' he said. 'Hi.' So *this* was who had won her heart. He smiled at Gloria, trying to hide his disappointment. 'So, which one is yours?' he asked, looking at the chicks.

'All of them,' replied Gloria, her eyes twinkling. 'This is our singing class.'

'Oh!' said Mumble, a small flicker of hope beginning to burn inside him.

'He teaches rhythm,' said Gloria, pointing to Seymour, 'and I teach the blues.'

'So you're not . . .?' Mumble began.

Gloria smiled. 'I guess I never heard the right song, did I?'

'That's great!' cried Mumble, elated. 'I-I didn't mean . . . ah, great for . . . you. I-I meant great . . .' He blushed. There was still a chance! he thought, as he hurriedly changed the subject. 'Well, I found out who's taking the fish! They're big and kind of ugly but – oh, Gloria – the things they can do. And they're coming here!'

'Is that so?' Gloria smiled kindly, the doubt tinged in her voice. 'So now you speak with them?'

'Well, they don't speak Penguin,' explained Mumble. 'But they seem to respond to this . . .' He gave a quick *tippity-tap-tap*. 'I suggest we all do it,' said Mumble. 'It really gets their attention.'

'And why would it do that?' asked Gloria curiously.

'Beats me,' Mumble said. 'But it works.'

Suddenly, a familiar voice boomed above the noise of the chattering crowd. 'SO YOU DARED TO COME BACK!' The crowd parted to allow Noah the Elder through.

'He says he's found Aliens,' said one earnest young penguin. 'And they're taking our fish. He says that they're coming . . . and that we all have to do *this*!' he said, demonstrating a little tap dance.

'THERE BE NO SUCH THING AS ALIENS!' thundered Noah.

The crowd was silent.

Beep . . . beep . . . beep.

'Er, Mumble . . .' said Gloria quietly. 'Turn around.'

Wordlessly, he turned, to reveal a large, beeping device stuck to his back. It had a small aerial and a blinking red light. Everyone stared, rooted to the spot.

'Is *that* . . . from *them*?' asked Gloria.

'Well, yeah . . .' Mumble said earnestly. 'But don't be afraid. I think it's a way to find me, that's all.'

'You led them *here*!' cried Noah. 'You turned them on your own kind?'

'Wait a second,' said Gloria. 'You just said there was no such thing as Aliens.'

Everyone swivelled round to look at Noah. 'Well, there's-there's not!' he stammered. 'But if there *were*, only a traitorous fool would bring them here!'

'But they have to come,' insisted Mumble. 'They're the ones taking our fish. They can do something about it.'

'Only the Great Guin has the power to give and take away,' Noah said.

'But the Great Guin didn't put things out of whack!' cried Mumble, feeling more frustrated than he ever had in the glass prison. 'The Aliens did!'

Then Noah really lost it. 'Beware, my brethren, the rantings of a fool,' he bellowed. 'For what a fool believes, no wisdom hath the power to reason away. So what you all must ask yourselves today is . . . who is the *fool* here?'

The crowd looked from Noah to Mumble, then back to Noah again.

Beep . . . beep . . . beep.

'Say, how does that feet thing go again?' a young penguin asked Mumble.

Mumble smiled. 'Oh, it's really quite easy,' he said, tapping out a few catchy steps.

He watched in growing amazement as more penguins decided to try it. 'That's right,' he said.

As the younger penguins started dancing, Noah and the Elders began chanting the phrases they'd always used to rule the group. 'Together we prevail . . . only we remain.'

Gloria joined Mumble and began to drum her feet. *Tippity-tippity-tappity-tap-tap.* Then the rhythm and excitement spread further, as Mumble's dancing infected more and more penguins.

'We remain. Only we remain!' insisted the Elders.

Gloria's singing pupils took to tap-dancing like penguins to water. Others started to try their own dance styles, more and more joining in, until the colony had transformed into a toe-tappingly wonderful penguin percussion orchestra. There were an awful lot of Happy Feet.

Far off, in the penguin suburbs, Norma Jean listened. 'Boys!' she called. 'You hear that?'

The Adelies appeared at once. 'Fluffy?' they cried. 'Tall Guy? Stretch? *Amigo?* Woo-hoo-hoo!'

The tap orchestra, led by Mumble and Gloria, rose to a deafening climax, while the Elders' chanting tried desperately to compete. The hearts and minds of some penguins still hung in the balance – this was a battle of the sounds. And, all the while, the beeping grew louder.

Norma Jean and the Adelies made their way through the swirling lines of dancers towards Mumble.

'Mumble!' his mother cried.

'Mama!' Mumble replied, overjoyed to see her. He spotted the Adelies too. '*Amigos!*' he cried.

They hugged and danced together, sur-rounded by Gloria and a frenzy of hysterical Adelies.

'We waited an' waited for ju!' said Lombardo.

'Wishin' and hopin' . . .' added Raul.

'. . . an' prayin' . . .' said Rinaldo.

'. . . an' hidin',' finished Nestor.

Ramon held Mumble extra tight.

But Mumble knew there was one more thing he had to do. 'Where's Pa?' asked Mumble.

Raul looked sad. 'Believe me, you don't want to see your deadbeat dad,' he said.

'Your pa is, sort of . . .' Norma Jean's voice was grave. 'Come and I'll show you.' She led Mumble into an ice cave. 'Memphis!' she called. 'Come on out of there.'

A forlorn figure emerged from behind a column of ice. 'Mumble, is it truly you?' asked Memphis, his voice low and croaky, as if he hadn't used it in a very long time.

'Every last bit of me, Pa,' said Mumble quietly, wondering where his bold, confident father had gone.

'Get over here.' Norma Jean's voice was soft and encouraging. 'Dance for your boy.'

'Oh, he don't need me,' Memphis said. 'He's doing just fine all by himself.'

'Come on, Pa,' urged Mumble. 'It's the

easiest thing in the world. It's just like singing with your body.'

Memphis didn't move. 'You'll have to forgive me, boy,' he sighed. 'The music's gone clean out of me.'

Mumble took a deep breath and tried again. 'It's just one big old foot after the other,' he said gently.

'Oh, I don't know,' Memphis said sadly. Then he lifted his head to look at his son. 'You show me.'

Mumble led him through some basic steps, and, ever so slowly, Memphis started to get the hang of it. 'That's right!' said Mumble as his father hesitantly *tap-tap-tapped*. 'You've got it!'

'Oh,' said Memphis, his eyes beginning to sparkle. 'I can feel it coming right up my legs . . . Oh, that feels *good*!' And, in a trice, he was dancing for real, adding a hip-wiggle here and there, making Norma Jean beam. Memphis was back!

Suddenly, the party stopped as a sound unlike any other came upon them: *chuppa-chuppa-chop-chop-chop-chuppa-chuppa*.

The sound was deafening, and with it a

monster appeared from the heavens, the creature's blades slicing the air, its bulk blotting out the sky. Everyone turned their attention to the great monster, watching as it circled above.

The Aliens had arrived!

And in the face of this overwhelming evidence, Noah could no longer deny Mumble's truth. Mumble rushed from the cave and saw that the black, whirring machine had landed. A group of humans were peering out at the great crowd of penguins. All of Emperor Land turned to Noah, and Noah turned to Mumble.

'I think you'd better dance now,' murmured Memphis.

And in front of the entire community and the Aliens, Mumble started to dance. First his family and the Adelies joined him, then a dozen more penguins, then a hundred, a thousand, then tens of thousands! Soon everybody was dancing, hundreds of thousands of Emperor penguins and five Adelies tippity-tappity-tippity-tap-tappity-tapping their hearts out!

The humans stared, awestruck. And then they clapped back.

Tappity-tap.
Clappity-clap.

The penguins and the humans were communicating!

As Mumble looked at the thousands and thousands of dancing feet, he tingled from the tip of his beak to the tap of his toes. He'd discovered where the fish had gone and the humans would bring the fish back. Emperor Land was safe, at last – and Mumble, the lone penguin who had stood up against a nation to follow his heart, completely and finally *belonged*.

In the middle of the star-studded velvety darkness of space, there was one very special star. Up close, the star was a brightly burning sun. And near the star was a blue-green planet, spinning round and round as if it would never stop. And right at the very bottom of that planet, in the coldest, cruellest land imaginable, is a most remarkable nation of beings who love, sing, and dance *with their hearts.*

If you look closely, you might find in the midst of the hundreds of thousands of penguins, Mumble and Gloria together, dazzling the world over with their happy feet.

And while one might think it was the Aliens who had saved Emperor Land, in truth, it was really the penguins, and one little penguin in particular, who had rescued the Aliens.

Of course, the Aliens would never know this. But if, for a moment, you looked at this remarkable nation from space, you would see and hear thousands upon thousands of fat and sleek Emperor penguins, all singing and dancing to the Heartsong and legend of the one penguin who had saved them all – MUMBLE!

Flippertastic Penguin Facts

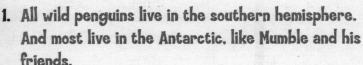

1. All wild penguins live in the southern hemisphere. And most live in the Antarctic, like Mumble and his friends.

2. Once penguins fall in love, they fall in love forever.

3. Emperor penguins lay just one egg. They rest this on their feet and cover it with a fold of skin to keep it warm and toasty.

4. Female Emperor penguins sometimes walk up to 160 kilometres to the sea in their search for food. And then they have to walk all the way back again.

5. Penguin chicks are covered in soft, downy feathers. As they get older, these feathers drop off to reveal the familiar black and white colouring.

6. Penguins may not be able to fly, but they can swim at 36 kilometres per hour underwater and leap from water on to land.